Honeysuckle

Honeysuckle

JP Bee

Library of Congress Control Number: 2020916729
ISBN: Softcover   978-1-6641-2848-4
               eBook   978-1-6641-2847-7

Print information available on the last page.

Rev. date: 09/04/2020

To order additional copies of this book, contact:
Xlibris
844-714-8691
www.Xlibris.com
Orders@Xlibris.com
818254

CONTENTS

Prologue.. vii
Introduction...ix

Chapter 1   The Basics... 1
Chapter 2   The Lost Years 8
Chapter 3   You Can't Go Home 12
Chapter 4   In Her Own Words: Memories Intact....................19
Chapter 5   Flashback: Relationships..................................... 30
Chapter 6   The Other Side 45
Chapter 7   I'm Here: The Seventh Day of My Rebirth........... 48
Chapter 8   The Move 54
Chapter 9   Florida Life and the Face of Death...................... 58
Chapter 10 The Rolling Hills (2000)..................................... 70
Chapter 11 Moving In.. 84
Chapter 12 Reincarnation 115
Chapter 13 Levels.. 120
Chapter 14 Luke's First Visit 123
Chapter 15 Open and Closed Minds......................................132
Chapter 16 My First Winter Back 134
Chapter 17 Questions and Answers..143
Chapter 18 Living Alone 147
Chapter 19 Ghost Busters... 152
Chapter 20 Revelation 159
Chapter 21 Costa Rica 165

Prologue

This book is intended to be entertaining with the possibility of exploring a different reality. It's the story of Augusta's life and death experience. It is not intended to disprove or prove any truth—just a possible revelation of something different. The events in this book occurred over this person's lifetime. It is written in the third and first person. The third person is used when her story is being told based on personal diaries, journals, and other people's memories of the events. The first person is when the memories are her own. The loss of early-childhood memories sparks and restarts a journey that opens the doors to hidden secrets along with passions, wisdom, and adventures, including astral projection, the ah-ha sense of the moment of time, spiritual activity, gifts, and the prompting of subjects, regeneration, and recreation of time.

The contents are not meant to attack anyone's religious or social beliefs and are not open to confrontation.

Introduction

Augusta grew up in a small suburban town in Connecticut. Raised as a strict Catholic, she was a middle child with two older sisters, one younger sister, and a brother. Augusta had a life full of structure. There was no boredom though she could not truthfully say that she could remember much about her life experiences since her car accident in 1989. The doctors clarified that due to a lack of oxygen in her brain, the head trauma she suffered destroyed a lot of her childhood memories; they were either lost or temporarily dormant.

She did have some memories, but the ones she was allowed to keep seemed to be left with her because they were to play a significant role in years to come. People and events she remembered were to be a part of her life and would be there for her to help or for them to assist her; all other people or incidents in Augusta's life that crossed her path or had no role in her future were, for the most part, forgotten and gone. Her immediate family did their best to fill in the empty years with memories as they knew them to be true. They also had a twisted sense of humor, making light of the situation. Augusta kept diaries and daily journals with exposed truths and secrets. If she believed everything her family told her to be accurate, she was born in a cabbage patch field, and her parents thought she was cute and different and felt a little sorry for her, so they decided to adopt Augusta and raise her as one of their own. They said that is why all her sisters had light hair, turned-up noses, and deep-blue eyes whereas Augusta had very dark brown hair with soft banana curls and hazel-green eyes. She might have believed them, but eventually, right after her sixth birthday, a baby brother, Joe, was born who had all the same physical characteristics that she did. They just took after her father's, Peter, Italian side of the family whereas her sisters leaned more toward the redheaded Irish side of her mother's, Carol, family.

Chapter 1

The Basics

When describing or introducing her children, her mother would get to her and say, "And then there is Augusta who we love dearly. She is a delightful child who tends to live in her world and march to her own music. If there is no music, she will sing and make her own. She has given us many challenges in life, and we are sure she will continue to make life interesting to all who are fortunate enough to be a part of her life."

Augusta guessed they were trying to compliment her with a little sidestep.

She would tell people that she never took her family's introduction offensively because they loved her and she was very comfortable with being different. She still could live among society, and she was even accepted by most. If someone did not like her but had no real reason not to, she felt a little sorry for them, for life was supposed to be lived and enjoyed, to learn and experience all the things and people that cross your path no matter how different they are from the norm or you. She believed you could learn something from everything and anyone no matter where they came from or how much education they did or didn't have because it is not by chance that you meet and remember everyone or anyone in your life. It is for a reason. Stop, listen, and learn.

Augusta relied on dreams and her sense of déjà vu to feel like she belonged to the rest of the world. After the automobile accident she suffered, Augusta made it her personal goal not to accept things at face value any longer. Just because she had been told or taught that something was right didn't necessarily mean it was or that it was the only truth. There can be many truths because the truth is in the person's perception. One hundred people can experience the same thing. Those 100 people could have different reactions depending on their knowledge and experiences. Thus, there are 100 different variations of the truth, and there is nothing sadder than a person genuinely believing that their way is the only way that everyone should think and be like them. She figured it made them feel safer and reassured them; they don't have to question themselves and the way they live their lives, and they don't have to worry that they might be wrong and have to change themselves. What a boring world we would live in if this were the case. Wars are started this way between nations and hate crimes run amuck. Religions divide, and judgment comes.

Augusta was like a newborn baby in her late twenties and early thirties. The few memories she was allowed to keep now had meaning after this. Everything happens for a reason, and she was about to find out why.

Her family could have taken this rare opportunity to remold her in many ways. Augusta knew they would never do that, and she guessed her original personality and what made her Augusta was still residing there deep inside.

She would remind people that the car accident in her life was horrible, but she thanked God every day that she was lucky enough to have experienced it. She would say, "I received a rare and valuable gift—the gift of sight and a new outlook on life—and like most gifts, they sometimes have to come with a price."

Very Early Years

Augusta did not have much to tell about her sibling years of interest because she just doesn't remember. She does remember not liking to go to bed; she was afraid she was going to miss something. Her brain would jump and wander, making drifting off to sleep a challenging undertaking. She would meditate. Of course, back then and being only a toddler who did not know what she was doing, she certainly didn't realize it was called meditation. She would not only meditate, but she would also go on journeys to all the places you would believe a small child would want to go and see. She remembers beautiful meadows filled with colorful flowers and rooms full of brightly colored balloons. She would fly in the sky over fields and rivers, gliding down to perch on treetops to gaze over the world. These were places she could visit only in her private world. She was never alone; she had a babysitter with her every time. She never told anyone back then that she would have these journeys and experiences. She was afraid they would say to her she was wrong or evil and try to make her stop; oh, how wonderful it was—it could not be wrong.

Her parents told her that they had to sleep with one eye open and both ears alert. As soon as she was old enough to walk, they would find her wandering around the house talking to someone or something several times a week. They said her little hand and arm stretched upward as if someone was holding it and leading her around.

Augusta could not articulate very well being so young, but they knew she was having a conversation with someone, giving short answers of yes, no, "I don't," "I won't go," "Don't wake Mommy!" Once they found her wandering around the front yard. Carol said, "Peter, how did she get out there? She is too small to have opened that door by herself, and is this the first time or has she had done it before?"

"I don't know, Carol, but let's put a lock across the very top of the door, so even if she stood on a chair, she would not be able to reach it to let herself out."

This sleepwalking, as they called it, went on for years, and they would just lead her back to bed. Her mother would ask her where she was going, and Augusta would say, "Home."

"You are home, Augusta."

"No, my other home, I like the smell of the flowers. See you," she would say to her invisible companion and fall back to sleep. Funny, Augusta did have a vague memory of an angel she named Jonathan who taught her to fly to those beautiful places she used to visit, and sometimes he would go with her on her journeys and keep her safe.

Teenage Years: The Tarot Cards

During her teenage years, she went through every day in a pretty standard way. She had to assume this was so because no one had mentioned anything outrageous or mind-boggling happening—just all the usual young teenager-type stuff one would expect a rebellious adolescent to encounter until she reached the age of sixteen.

Augusta had a sweetheart during her high school years. His name was Weiss. He had an older sister named Joan who frequented an elderly German woman who subsidized her social security checks with a little Tarot card, palm, and tea-leaf reading. She did not advertise the business, and it was strictly word of mouth, and from what was known, she was very sought after and had an outstanding reputation. It seemed that at the end of one of Joan's readings, the older woman told her to please bring the girl with the long brown hair to her very soon; she needed to speak to her. When Joan asked which friend, the woman just repeated in a trancelike voice, "Bring the one with long brown hair. She is very close to you."

Thinking of several possible candidates, Joan started to bring them by to meet the older woman who opened the old apartment door every time, saying, "No! That is not the one."

Joan then came to Augusta. "I have to bring you to meet my fortune teller this week. She has been asking me to bring her someone that matches your description, and you're the last one left, and she seems so desperate. Will you come with me?"

Augusta was curious to know if she indeed was the one the older woman needed to see. She, of course, agreed to go and wanted to do so immediately. They drove up to the apartment complex, and as they turned into the driveway, the German woman named Hilda was shuffling out to meet them. She moved quite fast for a woman of her advanced age with her slippers and stockinged feet, and she had such a look of relief on her face when she approached Augusta's side of the car. "My dear! Come in. Come in. I have been waiting for you. Joan, could you please come back in about one hour to pick up your friend? I would like to be alone with her if that is all right."

Joan looked puzzled but pleased with herself that she was able to complete the task that her old friend had requested of her. Augusta was just a bit scared, very curious, and worried about the woman wanted with her.

They entered the house, and it was not what one would expect at all. The walls were dark with very few knickknacks scattered around like you would expect to see in a grandma's house. The bargain basement furniture inside filled the rooms sparingly. Hilda led Augusta into her bedroom to a small bare card table. The room was filled with vases of honeysuckle flowers scattered around, and the scent filled the room. She reached over the table and grasped both her hands in hers. "Don't look so frightened, my child. I will not hurt you. When you leave, please take some flowers with you as they belong to you."

Her accent was so thick that Augusta thought she might have a hard time understanding what it was she wanted to tell her. She said nothing, just listened.

Hilda immediately reached for her deck of cards. Augusta never saw a card deck like these before; these cards were ancient and worn. Hilda immediately asked Augusta to handle the cards for a while. She said she would do a standard reading for her just to give some helpful information and to help her relax. She said she did not need to read the cards to know the reason she was there. "You have the gift as I suspect. So does your mother and hers before, and as I do, my child, and your life will be full of questions and answers unlike any others. You have something calling you. You should listen."

In her reading to Augusta, she said some things that were related to her family and future career. She told her that she would not end up with her current boyfriend, Weiss; she didn't' even flinch or try to console Augusta in any way even when it was apparent that the news of not being with him bothered Augusta immensely. It was just a matter of fact. Hilda chuckled and said, "Believe me, child—your path of life has no place for this young man. His purpose here is not yours, and it is just not in the cards."

The standard reading was over. Hilda gathered the cards together and pushed them across the table to Augusta and placed both her hands over them. "I am supposed to pass these cards on to you. I have to go on a trip soon, but I could not leave until I found you. You may not know what to do with the cards right now or even understand anything to do with this visit today, but you will someday, and they will be one of your learning experiences. Take the cards and keep them wrapped in a dark silk scarf, and someday you will know when to take them out and when to put them away and discover some of your gifts. Don't let the people who do not understand you keep you silent. Go now. I am tired, and Joan has come back to get you."

How she knew that was a mystery to Augusta because she was facing the window that viewed the driveway. Hilda's back was to it, and you could not hear the sound of the motor through the concrete walls.

"Augusta, don't worry about all the little things that will seem to hurt you over the years to come. They have their own meaning. Don't waste your time or energy on them when you have much more critical and fantastic tasks to face. It is your choice to take this information with you. How you handle the adventures to come is all up to you. Nothing is expected or written in stone. You do have the free will to choose and find your own way."

A week later, Hilda died, and Augusta put those cards away. She put them where she knew they would be safe. Augusta wondered if that was what Hilda meant by having to go on a trip. Was she going on a one-way trip?

Augusta did break up with her boyfriend Weiss a few years later, and it was her doing. She woke up one morning and was not at all satisfied with the practical life she would be living if she stayed with him. He was in love and only one year out of high school himself and was ready to ask her to marry him soon after her own graduation. She just felt no emotion for the relationship anymore and was restless and had so much she wanted and needed to do. If she stayed with him, Augusta knew she would stay content and would not search for any other possibilities. Augusta believes she broke his heart for a long time. Much later in life, she felt the pain he felt when he had a chance to break her heart, but it was one of the things she was supposed to experience and learn. Today he is thrilled, happy, and thriving with a family of his own and lives and works in the area where he grew up.

Chapter 2

The Lost Years

This time was one of the most robust memories Augusta had lost. She verified most of the events through her friends and family and in the extensive journals she always kept. Augusta left home in the summer of 1974, seeking independence at the age of eighteen, and had a couple of small apartments shared with some friends. Augusta became distant from her family and was lost and confused like you would think most young adults were, but she knew things that one should not have any reason to know. She stayed close to her younger sister, Beth, who told her that she was so afraid to get close to anyone because she would know things about them, like if they were going to die shortly or if someone was dangerous or evil. Almost everyone had a secret plan when they acted like they were your friends.

Augusta had a tough time with love relationships because most bored her to death. Her partners were like an open book, and she intimidated them to no end. The only young men who stayed around were usually brilliant bad boys who found her to be a challenge. She saw people in the form of energy, and it was either a warm or cold energy that would attach to her or draw the life from her. She could not stay in a room with certain people. She would just get up and leave, not offering any explanation and in a seemingly rude manner. Her sister knew what she was doing and why, and she knew it didn't faze Augusta in the least. If she did need to exit, it most likely meant that others should also exit because they were in the company of either evil or negative energy that was looking for a life light as Augusta would explain it.

It was during this period that she met Ed. He was the person she allowed to drain her energy over and over again. He was the one who offered and gave Augusta many of the things that she desired. It was like they had a heroin addiction to each other. They were both trying to break apart over the years but still found their way back to each other as though they had no say in the matter. Ed attacked anyone who seemed to get too close. For many years, he would stay within draining (energy) distance, but he knew his time with her was limited, and he often reminded Augusta that she knew he was a terrible person, and it was her choice to stay with him.

Ed called her a witch, the sweetest and most terrifying girl he'd ever met. They had an on-and-off relationship for years before the learning process, and the reason for having him in her life and Augusta in his had come full circle, and he was losing ground.

Also, during this time, she had a best friend. They spent most of their days together—attached at the hip. Her name was Anne. Anne had her gifts, but they leaned more toward the dark side; however, she tolerated Augusta and accepted her differences. Drawn to each other, they had such fun, and their times together were very intense. Augusta told her sister that when they were together, the most bizarre events would occur, and they, of course, found them exciting and worth exploring. They went just a little too far one day. Anne knew about the tarot cards and was constantly prodding Augusta to take them out and use them. Augusta had heard from many others that such things would open doors that she may not want to be opened if she was not ready to handle them, and the line that one walked between good and evil was fragile. Augusta was afraid at this point, not knowing if she was good or evil. Both seemed to reside in her, never allowing either one to take over, but Anne wore her down, and the cards came out. Augusta unwrapped the deck from the navy blue silk scarf, and she felt electrifying energy shooting through her body; her heart raced and was on fire.

She went into a trancelike state and, robotically and demurely, instructed Anne to hold the cards and lay five faces down on the table. Anne, being completely taken aback by her commands, immediately obeyed and placed five cards face down. Augusta turned the cards over like she was on a mission with no control or thought of her own.

The first one was flipped over, and she belted out, "Beware of things to come if you don't change the path you are going down."

The second card turned over made her say, "204, 204, pain, pain."

The third card said, "You will betray me," and the fourth card said, "No, he will not. He will die face down in a ditch. She will marry LB."

The fifth card . . . Augusta got violently ill and threw up part of the dinner they had just eaten and never told Anne anything about the fifth card.

Anne was upset and was not prepared for such a reading. She didn't get to ask any questions; although the cards spoke of her, all the information offered was about Augusta it seemed, and she felt as though it was a personal attack. It was Augusta saying those things, but it was not Augusta. She had no idea why she would say Anne would betray her; she loved Augusta and would never hurt her, and Augusta had no idea what 204 meant, not a clue. Anne said she had only a passing thought if Augusta would end up marrying the on-again-off-again love of her life, Ed, and what would happen to him and who Augusta would marry. Her passing thoughts came through the cards as no, she will not marry him—he will be in a ditch facedown, and Augusta will marry someone with the initials *LB*.

After they cleaned up the supper from the floor and had time for the whole experience to settle, they had a good laugh about the LB part. The only person they knew with the initials *LB* was Larry Broad who was as gay as the night was dark. The tarot cards were put away; Augusta didn't think she was quite ready to handle them at this point in her life, and they had to be evil or at least darkness around Anne.

Augusta did do many more readings later for people throughout the years and had to once again put them way because her accuracy was so outstanding that people used them as a crutch and did not want to start their days without calling on the phone to get a fix.

It was several years later when Anne's marriage was on the rocks that she pursued an affair with Augusta's casual boyfriend at the time. Lying and hurting were both involved. She lost Augusta's trust, and they parted ways and did not speak for a long time until Augusta heard she was deathly ill in the hospital with some sort of a virus that was attacking her liver and kidneys. She had to go and see her.

As she entered room 204, Anne was wailing, "The pain, so much pain! Please make it go away!"

Anne's marriage ended; the man she betrayed Augusta with dropped out of the picture as soon as her marriage was over, and he told her he was only using her. It was sad because Anne was very hurt. It was a waste because Augusta did not really care that much for him anyway and should not have allowed something so insignificant to get in the way of their friendship. It was a lesson learned.

Augusta was glad she did not remember that one. Reading the events in her journal sounded like a terrible time in her life. It was many years later when Augusta did have her memories intact that she learned of Ed's death. He had become an alcoholic and heavy drug user and was found in the streets of Bridgeport, Connecticut.

Chapter 3

You Can't Go Home

Augusta had a short-lived first marriage to a local boy. For a short time, they had a good life together. She made a good living, and for a while, they were, for the most part, happy.

They met when Augusta was bartending in a popular local pub in Connecticut. He was a musician by night and had a white-collar job by day. They had similar interests. He was charming and very talented, and she fell for him almost immediately. They ended up getting married and having a daughter Tabitha, during this time, Augusta wrote down every detail about her marriage, or should she say nightmare in her journal. She wrote it down for her mother who wanted her to have her marriage annulled in the eyes of the Catholic church. She never did turn those details over to the church, but writing it all down proved to have immeasurable benefits.

She was desperately trying to escape the emotional and physical threat posed by her soon-to-be ex-husband. Augusta and her daughter moved back to her parents' house so that they could feel safe and regroup.

She forgot that her parents were living their own marital nightmare. This memory was like a dream to her. She relived it in her mind like a broken film with a lot of worn-out holes, but it was verified to be true. Her father had always been a drinker, self-medicating himself because of war injuries and a life-threatening ladder injury he had suffered in past years.

As children growing up, Augusta and her sisters had no clue about the abuse their mother had taken when he was in one of his drunken stupors. Their younger brother and Augusta experienced a lot of beatings because they were outspoken and rebellious, which only provokes an alcoholic. Her mother did her best to shield them from most of what was going on until one day their father went off the deep end and into no return.

However, this house was still safer for Augusta and Tabitha than being with her present husband. She had gone home for a reason—she was supposed to go back not only for her and her daughter's safety but also for her mother's. Augusta thought things were better for her now that all the children had moved out, starting lives of their own. Everything gave the appearance on the outside things were good when the rest of the family would visit for gatherings and holidays. Who knew what was going on behind those closed doors?

Augusta's dad was a decent person but never should have had five children. He had suffered from multiple life-threatening injuries in the Korean War and had PTSD as well as other injuries throughout his life. Peter was a provider with many mouths to feed, which proved to be challenging. He loved Augusta's mother maybe too much, escaping early in life into the bottle. Peter went that day to the pub, a place he frequented unknown to Augusta but not to her mother. He stumbled home late that afternoon. Augusta was downstairs in the finished basement, where she set up a little apartment for herself. Her daughter slept upstairs on the second floor with her mother because they felt the cellar was too damp for anyone to sleep in. Still, Augusta was of course determined to have her own space, and they didn't bother to fight with her over it but would not allow their granddaughter to spend too much time down there, for example, sleeping.

That weekend Tabitha was visiting her other grandparents and was not home, thank goodness. There was a private entrance to the basement space, and it was void of normal noises that came from the rest of the house. However, this was not normal! There were loud crashes and screams and banging of several doors. As Augusta ran upstairs to see what was going on, she saw pictures that had once hung on the walls smashed with broken glass and frames on the hallway floor and lamps overturned in the living room with trails of blood that led to the den. There was a trail of bloody footprints and a bloody handprint going up the stairs to the second floor.

She froze in fear of what she would find when she got to the top. She yelled out, "Mom! Mom, where are you? What's happening?"

She heard fast running footsteps coming from her mother's bedroom door as she opened it and screamed, "Run, Augusta! Run here quickly."

Without even hesitating and never hearing such fear from her mother's mouth, she ran with her heart beating and her breath gone! What could be happening? Was there an intruder? Whose blood was splattered throughout the house. *My God what is happening?*

She made it to her parents' bedroom door. She could hear her father singing from the den downstairs, "Where are you, Carol the Barrel? You can't hide from me, bitch! Carol the Barrel, I am going beat the shit out of you!" He had no idea Augusta was home, or she would have never heard him sing the degrading drunken stupor name "Busty Gusty" that he would sometimes call her when he was drunk. He was stumbling through the living room, getting closer to the stairs, and the song he was singing was getting louder and more threatening as she heard and felt his steps thumping closer to the stairs.

Her mother opened the door and pulled Augusta inside. "We have to hide," she said. "Your father is in a crazy drunken state again. I hide here." She opened the storage room, which was called the attic. "He doesn't find me here."

There was not an actual attic, but as children, these second-level rooms were what they always thought of as the attic. The storage room went through to the other bedrooms with a crawl space just big enough for a person to pass through if they stayed on all fours. Her mother pulled some storage clothes, which were conveniently piled there, over them, and they tried not to make a sound as Augusta's father kicked the bedroom door open, singing his song again. Their hearts were beating fast and so loud that Augusta was sure he would hear them if he stopped singing and stumbling around for a few minutes. The closet door opened; they could listen to him riffling through all the clothes that hung there and pushing them from side to side, tossing shoes across the room. "Where are you, bitch? I know you are here."

He was in the closet next to the storage room but had not yet reached where they were hiding, but they knew that was his next stop. Would he be coherent enough to search in the crawl space? Would he be agile enough to crawl in after them? Augusta looked at her mother, saw the terror in her eyes, and knew she had lived this nightmare before. He was in the storage room now, breaking everything in his path. She could see his feet in the dim light that came through the small storage room window, and then she felt something brush up against her pants leg and heard a squeaking sound. She hated mice. Oh my god, she knew not to scream, but it came out anyway, and his feet turned toward the crawl space, and he sang, "I got you now, bitch."

They threw the clothes off that were concealing them and crawled as fast as they could to the other side of the space that connected to the second upstairs bedroom, praying that the storage room door on the other end was not locked so that they could escape through it and make their way down the back stairs to safety. He was closing in on their heels, but because he was drunk and so much larger than they were, he was having a hard time maneuvering his way through the close quarters. They reached the second bedroom storage door, but there was very little light in this part of the space because there was no window and one could not stand up here—the only thing that helped was a thin strip of light under the doorway that shone through from the dim late-afternoon light coming from that bedroom. Augusta fumbled to find the doorknob.

Thank God they found that the door was unlocked, and they quickly began to crawl out, trying to slam the door behind them, but he was faster than they thought, and he grabbed Augusta's mom's ankle, singing, "Carol Barrel, I FOUND YOU, AND I GOT YOU THIS TIME!"

Augusta grabbed hold of her mother's leg and pulled her clear, screaming, "DADDY, stop it! Stop it!"

He was shocked for a split second, realizing Carol was not alone. He was startled just long enough for Augusta to free her mother and head for the door that led downstairs.

Augusta and her mom headed for the kitchen, where they had hoped to escape. When Augusta had arrived home that day, she had entered through the basement. Therefore, she had bypassed the kitchen and had not seen the damage. An overturned table and chairs and broken glass everywhere now blocked their intended escape route. The surface of the linoleum floor was streaked with blood. She looked at her mother for signs of fresh wounds but found none and realized it was her father's blood and not her mother's.

Nobody could run or hide this time as he came into the kitchen. Carol raced to Augusta to cover her child instinctively. Peter spun and launched a wild blow at her mother's head. Her mom was now unconscious in a pool of blood.

The room began to transform when Peter approached Augusta to do as he had done to her mother. Just as she thought she was about to become a statistic and join her mother soon, she felt a comforting warmth surround her. There was a familiar sweet faint scent of honeysuckles filling the room. She experienced a bright light like a shield covering her from her father's first failed punch, which would have surely killed or seriously injured her if it had made contact with her face. His blow could not make contact, and he groaned as if his hand was broken, but by what? Then a voice that her father heard came directly from her mouth. "It is not your time. You have the power. *Use it!*"

She felt a surge of electricity run through her body; the fear that controlled her was gone. It was replaced by rage and self-survival. Her father stood, shocked by what had just occurred, but he quickly seemed to snap out of it, not believing what he had seen and heard. Charging at Augusta, he grabbed her by the neck and raised her up from the ground, moving her to the refrigerator door where she dangled. She saw the hate confused with love in his eyes, and she knew he did not want to kill her; it was like he was someone else, not her dad.

Next to the refrigerator was a drawer that held a set of carving knives. She had no idea they were there but was reaching for anything to stop the strangling. He was begging and taunting her to make him stop. It was like he had been possessed by someone or something. He was crying at the same time that he was choking her.

Augusta grabbed a large knife and raised it to his neck and said, "I will slice your throat if you don't let go."

He looked into her eyes and understood that his daughter would do it. He let go, and she fell to the floor. He stumbled backward, giving her just enough time to grab the phone to dial 911, and then he came at her again. The phone crashed off the table onto its side. The call went through, and she can only surmise that the operator could hear the ruckus on the other end. As he charged at her again, the strange energy field surrounded her once more—this time throwing him across the room on to the broken glass that covered the floor. He looked up at her in horror and, for a minute, seemed to be shocked back to his senses. He got up off the floor with blades of glass stuck in his back and jammed into his feet and left the room, leaving a trail of blood behind him.

Augusta ran to her mother who still lay motionless on the floor, trying to revive her before the possible next round of violence occurred. The sounds of sirens and police cars in the distance were getting closer. Reaching the door was not an option for Augusta who was overcome with weakness as the energy force that saved her twice drained her to the point of pure exhaustion.

The door was being axed down by the police from the other side, and they entered the decimated kitchen. Augusta recognized her Uncle John, the first officer on the scene. Augusta knew him immediately, and he asked where her father was. She pointed down the hallway. With guns drawn, her uncle and another officer moved in the direction she pointed while another officer called for emergency assistance on his walkie-talkie.

Her father appeared fully dressed in his fireman's uniform with all his medals of honor attached to his jacket as well as white gloves, hat, and dress shoes over his bleeding feet. He stood at attention, addressing the armed officers. "I am ready to go now," he said as if he was now a captured prisoner of war.

Augusta's dad was hospitalized for several months and dried out. Augusta stayed with her mom during this time to help her through the months ahead and to heal emotionally. They became terrific friends. They were more than mother and daughter now; they were closer than they had ever been. Still, her mother chose to make excuses for her father's insane, violent behavior because she had been dependent on him. He was not always like this and had fond memories of the years filled with love before alcohol defined him. Despite the abuse she had endured over the years, she still loved him.

Augusta went to see him in the hospital and did try to speak to him, but he would have nothing to do with her. He claimed he had no memory of the incident, but she knew that was not entirely true. She knew there were memories of what had happened that day. Her dad might not have known the details, but indeed he knew there was a force that stopped him. He was afraid of her like so many others before and did not understand but wanted to believe that he just imagined the whole thing. Sometimes she even wondered if it really happened herself.

They did not speak to one another for years. He would quickly find an excuse to leave the room once she entered.

Flashback: The Accident

Working as a car salesperson at a local dealership, Augusta was given a demo car to drive as one of her perks. This vehicle was a Geo Tracker. One morning while driving her daughter Tabitha to her sister Beth's house, who watched her during the day, she turned left onto the same street she had taken every day for months before. This time, there was a car that had stopped short just fifty yards from the turn because another vehicle was turning into a parking lot. This was a horrible design for a parking lot entrance to be so close after a significant intersection turn. The car in front of her stopped abruptly. She also did with much difficulty. The car behind her did not stop. It hit Augusta's car with such force that it bent in two and moved at least two car lengths.

She found out later that the older adult driving the car had panicked when she saw that a vehicle had stopped abruptly, and instead of putting her foot on the brake pedal, she hit the gas. Augusta climbed out of the shattered window to reach her daughter, placing her on the grass a few feet from the mangled car, and then passed out.

She drifted in and out of consciousness for days in the hospital, never saying anything. Augusta said she could remember the dripping noise of the IV line and the hissing sound of the oxygen tank as well as the muffled voices of people asking her if she could hear them. Augusta was in great pain, and she just wanted to make it all go away. The morphine was not working; it was only making her sick, and it felt like bugs were crawling all over her. She could not move her arms or neck. She could not speak and didn't know if she was broken or paralyzed or going to live or die.

Augusta's family stayed by her side, reassuring her that everything was going to be all right and not to give up fighting.

Chapter 4

In Her Own Words: Memories Intact

I spent about three weeks in the hospital recovering, my family always by my side. My memories are intact from this point on.

I have full memory of the journey and the experiences that have brought me into the present day. Like the blink of a tired eye, it seems that I knew for a few minutes, or maybe it was a split second, what mattered, and I understood the answer to "What is the meaning of life? What was my purpose?"

I wondered what all the fuss was about and why people made their lives so complicated, feeling empty and unfulfilled and hopelessly lost forever. It seemed so silly that one would just awaken to such a revelation without having previous knowledge of such vital issues. I grinned at myself. I experienced a moment of peace and utter joy. I was jerked back to reality by a burst of isolated pain in my right arm, triggered by my matronly-looking nurse sticking a massive thick syringe into my already-battered and abused vein. I wondered if maybe I knew this peace earlier in my life, but I just forgot that I knew.

Something didn't feel right. My blood vessels seemed to move and collapse deep inside, and the pain should have subsided by then, but it was getting worse. The nurse had slipped out of the room like something pending or more exciting waited for her. She was long gone when a warm feeling of liquid around the base of the needle, which was flat and taped against my arm, erupted like a blast of lava made of red blood shooting up into the air and headed toward the ceiling of my hospital room. The pain was gone, but I was so weak, and I just remember seeing a man I thought was my dad entering the room to save me. He never spoke to me. He smiled and held pressure on my arm to stop the rushing blood, rescuing me. He said his name was Jonathan, and when I looked again, he was gone and had been replaced by a now-very-attentive doctor.

My road to recovery was to be a long one, and I spent most of that time back at my parents' home. Home—though it was always a difficult place for me to be, it was better now. I did not have those awful memories I read about in my diary. Dad had stopped drinking and was in recovery; he was not as angry with me anymore though he still would not speak to me. I should say he was not as mad with the world. Mom was always caring and loving, and though he had a hard time showing it, Dad loved me even more.

I knew who almost everyone was in my immediate family, minus some; much of the details of my life with them were an empty void. I had empty blank black spaces where childhood memories should have filled me with the reassurance that they would keep me safe and protected from any lurking danger that might be behind closed doors. This was replaced with uncertainty and innocence. It was very unsettling and disturbing to me and more so to them. Everyone felt I needed protection and shelter.

I learned quickly to pretend that I indeed remembered many of the memory-lane stories I shared with them because their memories became mine even if they were as recent as yesterday, and not twenty years earlier. It made them happy, and it served me no purpose to squawk like a parrot over and over again, "No, I don't remember."

I had only vague memories of that day with my father and the strange energy force that was with me and protected me. My mother said I had a guardian angel that day. It was a movie rerun in my head—more like a horror show—and the remote was missing to change the channel. The rest of that time and the events that took place then were filled in for me by my mother in later years.

When I got more energy, my daughter and I moved into a little studio apartment above a convenience store in the area. I was still fragile, and my memories were full of holes and blank spots. The doctors still had me on quite a high dosage of steroids, which they claimed was a necessary evil during this time of my life. It seems that while hospitalized, I received an enormous amount of steroids to assist in my recovery. The accident that put me there had ripped the majority of my upper-body muscle mass, and at the time, these steroids kept things functional. So they claimed. I don't believe today this would be the medical practice of choice, knowing what they know today of this awful drug.

Working was not an option during this time. I was receiving state assistance, and my previous savings contributions to that fund provided us a roof over our heads and the necessities of life without help from others. I was determined to move forward and be on my own again. I was not going to allow this accident and my limited memories rule me. I had no car, nor was I allowed to drive either even if it was possible. I had a great fear of leaving the apartment. They say that it sometimes happens to a person after they have had a bad experience like mine. Selective memory loss—you almost choose to forget as a way of survival. You realize your mortality to an even greater extent in such situations. All the past life experiences and wisdom acquired over the years that would have made me comfortable walking among strangers were gone now. Maybe people I saw and talked to were not strangers at all, only to me. I thought perhaps they would be insulted if I did not acknowledge them as I passed by on the street or throw them a warm jest as I had always done. Maybe worse than that, they were terrible people who had done me harm at one time or another, and I had no way to know to stay away. All this was no longer clear and very frightening. I approached every new door that opened as a reluctant curious child, wondering if I might burn my hand on the hot stovetop or in the unprotected light socket in which I stuck my finger.

It took several weeks' work from my sister Beth and my brother-in-law Richard to get me out my front door, down the steps, and into their car just to go for a ride. I eventually did make my way back to the living, but it was a long hard road. I learned to smile at everyone who passed by, decided that even if they had done me wrong in the past, everyone deserved a second chance and another look, for maybe it was my own doing that I prejudged them before. I was no better than whatever evil deed I imagined they might have inflicted on me.

It was then that life came at me fast, or it might have just been the first time that I was alert and awake to a whole new world, and I was from that point on nicknamed Smiley. I was still residing in my little studio apartment above a convenience store, where I would work for cash under the table occasionally to give my daughter a little more than the basics that state aid allowed. The owner of the store took a liking to me and understood my situation and, for some reason, trusted me completely. If I could work, great. If I couldn't, it was not a problem. The apartment was not far from Tabitha's school and was right down the street from my ex-mother-in-law. Although I was no longer married to her son, we stayed very close and spent many hours together as if we were the best of friends. I would get tired very quickly and would have bouts of pain that would place me in bed for days on end. I refused to take any more pain medication because it only messed up my head and didn't give me relief. However, against my better judgment and wishes, I was instructed to ingest steroids by my doctor. They told me I had to continue because now my body could not produce antihistamines. I was allergic to the air around me. Stay on the steroids or live in a bubble; that was my choice.

There were many nights that I just wanted it all to go away. I would daydream of a forever release. I prayed for a solution to my agony and maybe sometimes thought about a possible way out. Now I started to understand the meaning of selective memory loss. I am thankful that I had enough sense not to take oxycodone because I am quite sure if I had not had a clear head, I would have found that forever release. At that time, I realized my body was in pain, but my head was clear, so why not detach the two and at least capture some temporary relief whenever possible? I had read about mind over matter, self-hypnosis, and meditation. Never gave them much thought in the past, but heck, I had nothing to lose and nothing more pending to do. I had no material to guide me, and the Internet at the time was not the knowledge highway it is today. Nor did I have a computer.

I decided to wing it. I had a memory that I was allowed to keep as a child of taking journeys to faraway places and an angel friend Jonathan who was there for me and how I longed to feel that glorious freedom again. If I accomplished this as a child, why could I not do it now?

I lay down on my bed, which was also my sofa, situated against the wall in my little apartment. My daughter was spending the weekend with her father—still under the court supervision of his mother—so there was no worry that my experiment or weird personal adventure might scare or harm her. This was my entertainment, escape, and hope.

I hadn't yet received permission to drive, and at this point in my life, I had only a few friends left. Anne was not around much, and my life friend Jill had married and moved to Florida. The four brick walls in my little studio apartment that imprisoned me could take me away for an evening of fun or adventure.

I experimented with many different ways of taking my mind away from the aching pain. I had to imagine that I was a head with no body attached because the pain was in the body. I lay very still on the bed, making sure that my limbs were not touching each other or my torso. I started with my breathing to relax in the most profound way possible. I began with breathing in deeply through the nose until my stomach rose then releasing the air into the atmosphere slowly and deliberately through the nose, not the mouth. Every breath I would take in, I would say, "In with the good," and with every breath out, I would say, "Out with the bad."

I repeated this silent chant over and over again. Once my breathing had become natural and flowing rather than deliberate, I started the process of detachment. I imagined that I had no feet. I visualized them gone, believing that there was nothing there to move, and as I tried to move them, they disappeared and dissolved. I mentally traveled up to my legs and repeated this process. Then I lay as just a stump in my bed. I had no legs and no arms, only my torso and my head.

Most of my pain resided in the torso. Imagining it wasn't there seemed daunting. I thought that instead, it might be easier if I imagined a small pinhole in the middle of my back. I could release all of my pain slowly from that pinhole with every breath I took. I made an escape route for the pain to leave. I had never tried anything like this before, and it was working. I felt a part of me departing my physical body first, rising to the ceiling in the room and then escaping out the roof and into the night sky. I was transported in a flash to a parking lot, which I recognized as the one outside a familiar motorcycle club. A man was face down in between a cluster of motorcycles, bloody and mangled. I had not seen Ed since the accident, but I remembered him. Ed could not deal with my physical and emotional trauma and never even made an effort to visit me in the hospital or look me up once I became stable. I did see him on occasion outside my apartment, parked or driving by several times a week, but he never stopped in.

Ed slowly turned over onto his back, groaning, coughing, and gasping for air when he sensed my presence. He reached out for me and called my name. I was so startled about not only that I was actually there but also because of the fact that he could see me. With those thoughts, I was pulled back into my body and sat up in bed. *Wow, what a trip!*

Fifteen minutes passed, and I heard a knock at the door. *Who could that be this late at night?* Through the peephole, I saw a stocky full-bearded man holding up Ed with both arms. "Open the door, Augusta. This bastard is heavy."

Obviously, this man knew me. I unlatched the door and stared into Ed's eyes.

"Sorry, Augusta," the man said. I might have known him in my past life, but his name was void to me now. "Ed insisted that I bring him here.

He is talking nonsense, something about you being a ghost. He probably has a concussion. He was beaten up pretty bad. Can I leave him here please?"

"Yeah sure, bring him in and put him on the couch. Does he need to go to the hospital for stitches or anything because I cannot drive him. I do not have a car."

"Yes, he probably should, but he doesn't want to go. You know there are drugs and alcohol involved, and God knows what else, so let him sleep it off, and he can deal with it himself tomorrow."

His friend left, and Ed looked at me and said, "You were there, right? I saw you, right?"

"Yes, Ed, you saw me."

He passed out on the couch, and when I woke up in the morning, he was gone.

I practiced this form of pain medication every chance I got. I preferred to be alone with my experiment than with people or the rest of the world. My space was so much more beautiful than theirs, and everything seemed so much clearer and uncluttered. That inner peace and all-knowingness that I had experienced in the hospital that day returned, and I liked it. This self-medicating method had to be the best drug in the world, and it cost nothing but determination and the absence of time. I would have many hours of relief, and I realized that there was so much more available to me if I could just keep going. I wanted to go to the next step, but I was not sure what that next step might be; however, I was so excited about the possibilities that I pushed the envelope.

The paramedics claimed that I was clinically dead when they found me. How long? No one knows. It could have been for a minute; it could have been a lifetime. I made my own decision to wean myself off those awful steroids, and the doctors said I put myself into cardiac arrest, and my body went into shock. They may be right, but I knew they were slowly killing me anyway, and this was my choice. I firmly believe this was the right thing to do. I do not know if I was dead. I think I just went to the other side for a visit for a while, and the body, because it no longer existed, was in reality by rights dead as we know death to be.

My heartbeat slowed down so much that it was virtually undetectable. I floated up and saw my body below as peaceful and lifeless as if I was in a profound sleep from which I could not be awakened. I did not care, and I wanted to go wherever I was headed, no turning back, but I was aware of a light beam, more like a string that was attached to the middle my back where I had imagined that pinhole escape route to be. The line was just effortlessly floating along with me toward a speck of light in the abyss. Was it a star or candle in a dark room or a street light that would get brighter as I entered its space?

As I entered into this vast open space, there was a hallway, a transparent beam of mist. I found myself walking down it. There seemed to be many doors on either side of the corridor—an infinite number of them. In the beginning, the doors were concrete and very real. I could sense familiar sounds and experiences behind them. There were voices of familiar laughter, thoughts of hunger, and visions of houses, cars, and acceptance. I had no desire to open any of them as I wanted to continue on the road toward that little speck of light that was getting bigger and bigger as I approached. As I pursued it, I noticed that some of the doors were enticing me to open them with promises of desired power, wealth, immortality, beauty, and most of all, no more pain forever. It was getting harder and harder to resist their alluring pull, but the light was so peaceful, so much more inviting, and it felt like the right path to take. The illumination was not trying to sway me one way or the other with the promise of grandeur. It was there for me to recognize the brightness. I knew it was my decision to proceed down this hallway or to step off and enter through one of those doors.

Ahead of me, a luminous figure appeared—not male or female but familiar like an old friend that I once knew—and I felt safe.

The entity asked me if I had any desire or wish, what would it be? My immediate thoughts were transmitted but not spoken—to be free of this pain and to be healed. I wanted knowledge but not necessarily the knowledge one finds in most books. I wanted an understanding that goes beyond that. I wanted to see the world as it indeed was and to recognize the truth when it hid from me. The entity pointed to a door that was as solid as any familiar wooden door. I was reluctant to open it because of fear. Was I allowing the fear of the unknown to rule me, or was there something not right? Did I have just cause to be reluctant?

I knew if I entered the door that the light ahead was no longer an option, but I also knew that I still had earthly desires and unfinished earthbound experiences pending that needed to come full circle. Was the entity trying to trick me into that doorway? Should I go? Should I not? However, for some reason, I felt safe with this old friend. I opened the door but did not step in.

Visions of the world as in a motion picture flashed before me. There was so much; it was so fast—too fast—and too much for me to absorb. I wanted to know what I was seeing. I realized I was feeling and seeing my life, many of my experiences, and other lives pass before my eyes. I was flying over rolling hills down upon a white farmhouse, a place I had seen before. I had been there before, but when? I knew I had to find it. I had a thought of my daughter with her beautiful face and loving eyes. Her arms extended to me as if she was intensely trying to reach me. I knew she needed me and how she also needed a good father figure in her life just as I needed a good man who was a friend to me and accepted us as we were. I needed a man I could trust and knew that both Tabitha and I wanted unconditional love, something I had not known for a very long time from my past relationships, and this was something I so wanted to be able to give my daughter. She saw only so much hurt and sorrow from me, and she deserved a chance to know more.

These are the thoughts that yanked that string of light attached to the center of my back taut like a fish line reeling me back into my body. As I was rapidly falling back to my own dimension, I was returning with knowledge. Not all, mind you. Because of fear, I only opened the door—I did not step in. I knew I would not entirely be healed, for I had to retain the memory of this beautiful gift I had received, and just a little bit of pain would be a constant reminder of that. I could handle that as a great gift. I knew my daughter would be happy and experience the love she so deserved because I was told within seven days, I was going to be able to show her by example.

I opened my eyes to my apartment to find Tabitha peering around the corner of her bedroom toward my direction. My mother and a paramedic were by my bedside. The paramedics were just about ready to zap me to restart my heart. I sat up in bed with a smile on my face and said, "What's going on?"

I was full of life, and I felt like I was reborn, back in my body. I noticed the expression of astonishment across their faces as though I was a visitor from another world. Over time I tried to explain to them my trip to the other side. Of course, they did not believe me and were not at all persuaded. Everyone said that my visions were just delusions and hallucinations from my dying brain. I knew they were mistaken, but because I would never again believe in only one truth, I accepted the possibility that their reality was as real as mine. If the death was what they understood, then so be it—*I had a death experience.*

I had brought back a lot of new knowledge with me that was not known to me previously, but when asked, "What was it like dying? What did you learn?" the answer that was most important to me was that we are all here to learn and that we have the gift of choice to learn whatever way we need to, and for as many years or lifetimes, it may take us to get to our final destination. The result for each of us will be the same; which doors we decide to open for arriving there just depends. The doors we know best and the doors that promise all the earthly desires we may have can be selected. That's all right because you had to reopen that door so the next time, you might know it, and you can pass it to go forward into the light or go through another experiential door that will allow you to learn the next lesson.

Some people take many lifetimes going through the same door, never learning from the choices they have made. I think we have given that the name of purgatory, where one is in limbo until someone gives them a handout or they finally wake up from their slumber and climb out. There are no terrible doors, right or wrong doors—they are all there and all different for each of us.

The final destination is the light, but because I am still here with you, I was not ready. I don't yet have the complete answer that people seek. I chose a door that brought me back to you, and maybe I am here talking with you because you are searching, and like the entity that helped me open a new door, I am your entity, here to help you the best way I can because you asked. If you were not ready to ask, I would not be talking to you. Maybe the next time, I will go a little further. I need to learn more, and here in this body is the fastest place to do just that. I will never be the person I was, and I take that as a gift, but I want to earn the right to more rewards. I want to learn.

There is no reason to worry about your past or past lives. There are no mistakes made or lost opportunities. Everything is the way it should be because you have made it that way. All choices have been yours and part of your learning experience, and lost memories are not lost because every time you enter a new door, you have grown, and there is no reason to look back. You are a unique being now with every new door you choose to open. It is your choice, and you are doing it to be where you are today.

I may have a desire to remember yesterday, but going back to regain those memories would just be a convenience and take me farther away from my destination. Therefore, I take it as a blessing that I have erased from my memory many yesterdays. I don't have that baggage to carry around as others do. Traveling to new places is so much quicker when you only have a backpack.

There is no need to be sorry or depressed about my lost memories because being without them allows me to get closer to that light faster. I know that I open doors that most people wouldn't dare to, and I walk alone most of the time. Once in a great while, I do come across someone who has traveled farther than me or someone behind me, and we support each other whenever we can.

I have learned to live in this world and dimension; one's feet must be firmly planted on the ground, steady and straight, attaching themselves to earthly material items. Only the strong survive among the competitive human race that will stop at nothing to possess power and wealth. We are beings with the capacity for great love and compassion, but we also have animal instincts to kill or to be prey. We are distrustful and closed-minded about something new or unfamiliar to us, so we project our fear on to others. We teach our children, insisting they believe and follow what we do. If they do not, like many otherworldly beings, they join forces with political and religious groups and families so they grow in large numbers.

When a person has the gift of sight or has been enlightened but still wants to be associated with this planet, he/she must be strong enough to walk alone most of the time until given the honor of meeting someone like themselves. The numbers are low, and these individuals choose to be invisible as they continue to hide and blend in, looking for the balance between the two worlds. They are not ready to step away from one world or the other completely. They are not willing to join the more-prominent material world but are not powerful enough to be separated or excluded. They wait patiently and instinctively know when they come into contact with another being vibrating at the same level.

Chapter 5

Flashback: Relationships

I was a big one for writing things down, and many of my journals that held experiences were misplaced or purposely hidden to be found at the appropriate time. Maybe this is the reason why and how I met my life partner. He was searching for a better way, not understanding the unbalance. I needed someone to ground me to earth because I was not yet ready to be banished from the human race. I returned to this earth dimension so that I could raise my daughter and help others searching for answers.

A very incredible part of my life was meeting my second husband and best friend—how the whole thing transpired still amazes both of us as well as anybody else who knows the story to be true. We were not supposed to end up together until the time was right. Together we have accomplished many dreams. We were an unlikely pair to find one another, but we did. It did not just happen; it was all in the cards. LB, the initials the tarot cards gave, were to spell out later in my life.

To understand the bizarre circumstances leading up to our relationship, let me recap where I was in my life at the time of our first and many encounters. I was about eighteen years old, rebellious, healthy, and attractive with green eyes and long dark brown hair that fell halfway down my back. I was of legal age then to drink and frequent the pubs and bars of my little hometown back then before the state of Connecticut, along with others, decided one should be twenty-one years of age to consume alcoholic beverages. I liked going to the fast-paced disco facilities, dancing and partying with my friends, many of whom were years older than myself. When I wasn't partying, I was playing my guitar and writing my music, which was a love that was introduced to me when I was about twelve years old by my father, Peter. He got me my first guitar and taught me my first song: Johnny Cash's "I Walk the Line." What a special memory I have, with my father sitting on the breezeway steps strumming that store-bought department instrument. I can still feel the steel strings cutting into my fingers as he placed them on the neck of the guitar to form a chord. There were only three chords required to make the song come together. Peter must have had the same love and need for music because he took the time to teach me, something he very seldom did with any of his other children. He helped me find a way to express my desire to learn and sing and write down all my feelings and convey them in songs.

It is funny how I retained this memory and no others. Or is it? I think he saw something in me, even back then, that was unsettling to him. I would spend hours day after day up in my room, practicing that one song he taught me until I got it perfectly. I played around with that guitar right up until my life-altering accident, but that is another story.

When not partying and dancing in the high-energy discos, I liked to visit a private club in which a member who paid a yearly fee could drink and converse at a fraction of the cost that public facilities charge. I knew the bartender Jerry, and he was more than happy to buzz me in when I announced myself over the intercom. I thought he might have a thing for me, but I pretended I was naïve about his attraction so as not to lose a friend by misleading him in any way and rejecting his advances. He enjoyed my visits, and I must have been a breath of fresh air among all those middle-aged and elderly members of thirty-five and older.

He encouraged my love for music and pleaded with me to bring my guitar and songs that I had written and entertained the members from time to time. "You owe me," Jerry would say. "You're not a member, but I let you in any way, and let's face it—you have to pay somehow for all the drinks you have never paid for. My customers would enjoy your music and entertainment, so tomorrow night, I will set up the microphone and give you a chair, and you will play for us."

Jerry knew unless he gave me an ultimatum, I most likely would have run away from the opportunity he was presenting to me. So I played.

I was not a good musician, just a good entertainer. I had a passion and was original, so we all had fun, and the songs I wrote were unique. People paid attention as if what I had to say mattered, and I was appreciative.

I particularly noticed an older man, at least five to ten years older than me, sitting at the bar watching me occasionally with a grin of approval. He was very out of place with his long blond hair, firm slender muscles, and large bright transparent-blue eyes. He looked too cool and out of his element to be sitting among the local patrons.

We talked, and he brought me many cocktails when I took my set breaks. I just know he told me a few things about himself, but I don't have any more memory of the conversation with him. I must have been comfortable because I allowed him to drive me home on his motorcycle that night, guitar flung over my shoulder and held by a strap. My on-again-off-again lover, Ed, was too drunk or cheating on me or most likely both to show up that night to bring me home. He was supposed to come and hear me sing, and he inspired many of the songs I wrote, but as usual, he was a no-show. I don't even know how I got to the club that night in the first place. I guess a girlfriend dropped me off. I know I needed a ride home, and Jerry gave me the go-ahead with his eyes, letting me know it was safe for this person to offer me that ride.

Luke was a good listener and let me babble on and on. I know he told me about how he was involved in music and bands, and he had been in the navy. Besides that, I don't believe or remember him talking at all. Neither one of us remembered what we talked about—not that it mattered. I was eighteen. He was an older man of twenty-four but seemed to be much older to me, and I felt safe with him. I put my arms around his waist and held on tight as the motorcycle hugged the back roads of New England. The night air was fresh, and I felt alive and free as he drove me to my home. He knew just where I lived. He slowed down as the house came into view but coasted past just a little to be out of view of the picture windows facing the front lawn and the street. He shut down the engine, and without completely getting off the bike, he turned around, straddling the bike and now facing me directly—my heart raced. He gently and quickly put his arms around me, pulled me closer to him, and kissed me perfectly. It was an "I like you very much" kiss. I know if I had been standing, my knees would have buckled under me, and I would have fallen to the ground like a wet noodle. That is all I remember, like a dream that you know was great but is gone on awakening.

I went back to the members-only club over the weeks many times, hoping to see him again and carefully interrogated Jerry many times about who he was and where he was because Jerry knew him. Jerry wasn't willing to give up any information about Luke, and I suspected it was because he was a little angry that I did not show interest in him the same way. The other issue was that Jerry was also a very longtime friend of Ed's, and there was probably some guilt involved caused by this loyalty. However, he didn't want me to with Ed either, knowing he was no good for me or any nice girl for that matter. Ed was a hound when it came to women, with a sex addiction that could not be satisfied. The sex was amazing.

Jerry was a very private and mysterious person, always thinking but usually silent, keeping his opinions and most thoughts to himself. I didn't want to hurt Jerry's feelings because I did wish I could be more attracted to him and hook up. After all, Jerry was such a decent guy who would most likely treat me like a queen, but it just wasn't there. I liked him. I would do anything for him but only as a great friend.

When Jerry saw that I was getting impatient with his avoiding responses, he finally blurted out, "Forget him. He's got a wife and a couple of kids."

My heart sunk—how could this gentle, seemingly caring, and loving man be married and flirt with me? The kiss was so pure and purposeful as if he had the right to crawl inside me. I was doomed to attract the scum of the earth. I couldn't think of it in my heart like that at all. He obviously was not happy or really just had a connection with me, and maybe he knew it was wrong, and that was why he was not coming by the pub any longer, or perhaps Jerry threatened him to stay away from me. I tried to come up with every excuse I could for him leading me on. Let's face it—I had a boyfriend also. Maybe I was not married, but I was just as wicked and unfaithful as he was. I was unhappy, so perhaps he was too and was just waiting for someone to help him walk away from his current committed situation.

While playing my next set, the love songs were more intense than earlier, with my heart broken and worn on my sleeve. He walked in. I tried to be calm, like his presence was acknowledged and welcomed, but prayed he could not see my heart pounding in my chest. I finished my set and walked up to him, sat down, and acted like he was a good friend I hadn't seen in a very long time and was just happy to see him again. He seemed a little different and distant, not as warm and inviting and interested in me as on our first encounter, and Jerry just kept shooting me looks of disapproval and, at the same time, amusement.

Jerry walked toward the microphone that was still turned on and announced that he would like to introduce a second entertainer that evening. "Luke, come on up."

Funny, I was fixed on him walking through the door. I didn't even notice that he was toting his guitar. I remembered he was involved in music; I must have missed the entertainer part. I must have just babbled all night about myself that evening. What a jerk I must have been. No wonder he stayed away so long. Any smart woman knows to let a man talk about himself and to shut her mouth if she wants that man to take an interest.

He was an outstanding musician, and his singing voice was fantastic—much better than my own. I felt like a silly groupie who was hooked line and sinker. I listened and watched and decided I didn't care if he was married and had a few kids. I was angry with Ed who was always cheating on me. I knew back then that there was still someone unfaithful to someone else. Those times sleeping around was expected and accepted—kind of a free-love attitude; it was just the way it was. If you liked someone, showing it in lovemaking was not that big of a deal. There was no AIDS or herpes, only crabs. The only question typically asked was, "Do you have protection, or are you on the pill?"

"So," I said, "Where are you playing? Can I come and see you? Maybe spend some time together?"

"Sure," Luke said, "I am playing next Saturday night in Hedge Brook at the Roadside Inn just off the parkway. Do you know where that is?"

"Yes, I think so."

Jerry stayed within earshot, pretending that he was washing glasses behind the bar, but I knew he was eavesdropping on our conversation, and as soon as Luke got up to leave and placed a little kiss on my forehead, Jerry said under his breath to me, "Augusta, he's not who you think he is."

He was annoying me right then; he wasn't my father. He was just jealous and overprotective. None of us is who we seem to be, and I felt at that point that I just wanted to have a good time, and before Luke, no one had taken my thoughts away from Ed in a very long time. Ed, the so-called boyfriend who treated me more like a pet he owned than his beloved. I was going to meet up with Luke and left Jerry smirking, shaking his head and muttering to himself.

It seemed like it took forever for the week to finish while I waited for that Saturday night to arrive. I told Ed I was going out of town to see my cousin, and of course, he seemed pleased because I am sure that would make it much easier to run amuck and whore around town with me not there. I told my parents I was spending the night at my best friend Jill's house; we covered for one another all the time. I packed an overnight bag and turned onto the parkway heading for Fairfield, Connecticut. I saw the red neon sign flashing ROADSIDE INN.

He was just starting his last set and almost seemed surprised to see me walk in. He took a fast break, abandoning the group of people he was sitting with to join me at my table. He looked at me bewildered—pleased with both himself and me—but confused. He asked me why I had come, and I quickly answered, "To be with you tonight."

It was strange. I wasn't as attracted to him as that first night. He wasn't as charming or warm as I had remembered or nowhere near as exciting as I had thought, but I was on a mission. My overnight bag was packed in the car, and I already had excuses for not going home, so I was staying.

He felt it necessary to tell me himself that he was married and had a few kids and was not from the area but traveled on the road a lot with his music. He seemed taken aback a little when I told him I knew that already but didn't care. I appreciated that he at least wanted to give me the choice of staying after he was honest with me, and that the night would be a solitary one.

I was okay with that as the morning sun came up. He was not who I thought he was. Damn, Jerry was right. He was just another man, nice and alluring, but I had no connection with him. I went on my way and never gave him another thought until many years later. It all made sense finally.

Through the years, Ed had drifted in and out of my life, and one night, when we went out together to a popular café called the Cross Street Café, there was a memory that I had and would hold forever. The pub was hopping, with groups of people drinking and talking and standing around. Ed took my hand abruptly and led me to a group of people to introduce me to one forbidding-looking guy in the middle of the pack. I mean, he had very long blond hair—clean but past the middle of this back—a full wiry mustache, and tie-dyed jean pants and shirt that were worn through at the knees and ripped at the pockets. His rough brown face with big blue piercing eyes peered out at me through the long blond hair that hung over his face. He had a soft voice, warm smile, and firm but gentle hands as he took one of mine in both of his to address me and said, "I am pleased to meet you, Augusta."

I could tell with only one articulated sentence that his appearance was the opposite of the man. "Have we met before?" I asked.

"Probably sometime in another life, so it is a pleasure to meet you again."

It was like slow motion took over all of a sudden. The room started to spin, and the voices in the pub became muffled. I turned to Ed for help, and he stood looking at me and said, "You are going to marry him one day."

Then as fast as things went whacky, all went back to normal, and Ed stood with a confused look on his face and said, "What and who are you? You scare me. It is like I have no control when you are around, and what the hell did I just say?"

I was beside myself about him telling me that I was to be with this guy. He was not my type and how rude for him to say such a thing to me when we were out on a date. Our relationship was never quite the same after that night. Ed was afraid of me. A six-foot-two, 200-pound man that intimidated most other men was fearful of me.

It had to be about six months or so later that I found myself out with Ed again at a dancing club downtown—not the safest place to be—but I went there often with Ed and felt stupidly comfortable. Ed quickly got drunk again and disappeared on me, leaving me in the babysitting hands of some of his friends.

I was sulking at the bar when I heard a voice ask me, "Where is your boyfriend tonight? Did you lose him, or did he lose you?" He was sincere and, at the same time, annoyingly sarcastic.

"Yeah, well, you know how it is. That's Ed. He'll be back, and he probably just stepped out for a minute. Have we met before?"

"Yes, you are kidding, right? My name is Luke, and we have met several times before. Don't you remember me? I gave you a ride home from the members-only club once, and Ed introduced you to me, and well, let's just say I know who you are, and I think you are too beautiful and too much of a lady to be with someone like Ed. Why are you with him anyway? He doesn't treat you like you deserve. You could do so much better."

"Oh yeah, I remember," I said as I nodded, ensuring him that I genuinely did. It was all coming back to me, and I was not too hard on myself for having a lapse in memory. I remembered him then; I just chose to forget the whole incident and never connected the encounters. I had fallen head over heels for the man who drove me home that night from the members-only club so many years ago. I had slept with him a week later and decided he was boring and not what I had expected.

I just wrote our intimate evening off as a one-night stand and remembered I was lucky that he was just dull and not a serial killer. I felt a little empowered that night cheating on Ed as he had on me so many times before. Therefore, even though I was sadly disappointed that Luke bored me to tears, I at least got something out of the evening. I never connected this person with the one Ed introduced me to at the Cross Street Café that night, the one I was supposed to marry someday. That's what he meant that night by saying we met in another life. *Oh, now I get it,* I said to myself.

How embarrassing that he avoided bringing up that Roadway Inn romp altogether. Maybe he was just polite. "Bartender, give the lady whatever she is drinking." He turned to me and said, "Do you mind if I sit down?"

Wow, he asked me. At least he had manners. Most guys were just pushy and assumed things they shouldn't. They would have sat down next to me whether I wanted them to or not, making me get up and leave after a painful chat. However, Luke might do for the company while I waited for Ed to return.

Ed did return and showed signs of jealousy that Luke and I were deep in conversation. He quickly led me away from my new friend. Luke, though strangely in no way intimidated by Ed, politely gave me a look of disappointment and left.

My family disapproved of Edward. We were a close dysfunctional family like most, and I was young, and he was an older man of twenty-five and drove a Harley motorcycle with a tribe of what they called thugs. He had a great job as a master plumber; his now-alcoholic father taught him, so he had money to burn in his pocket at all times. He was very popular in his circle and was a very intimidating man who loved women, and they all adored him, including me. He had no inhibitions when it came to sex and was more than willing to teach me the ropes. He showed me things, and we did something that I now know was not the norm, but at the time, I just assumed everyone made love this way, but that was as far from the truth as could be. He was six foot two and had a body that was 200 pounds of muscle that I could not put my two hands around. I was five foot two and 110 pounds, and he would maneuver me around like a rag doll. Once you made love to Ed, the rest were mincemeat. He had a way of destroying your experience with any other poor slob who thought he knew what women wanted and needed. Seduction was his talent and his calling card. That's what made all of my competitors come back for more. He was addicting, and because you could not get a fix or high like his anywhere else, women would have to wait their turn for him to come back around when ready, and they made sure they were there. He was a master at juggling all his affairs. He was a god in the eyes of all his male friends who would ask, "What does he have that makes you take all his shit?"

How do you explain that to another man? They all wanted to be around him as much as the women did because he would leave broken hearts and addicted clients everywhere, so his male cohorts would all be too willing to stand close by to pick up his discarded casualties. Many of his "toys" would try another man, but most would wreck their new relationships by not being able to break their damaging patterns with Ed. If he had flirted enough, tempting them sufficiently because it had become a game, they would become addicted to the Ed drug just by being offered another fix.

I was his girlfriend or his possession, so everyone would remind me that that Ed kept a close eye on me, never allowing me to even think about being with another man. If he thought one of his male companions was getting a little too close to me, he would shut them down fast. I became their little sister, and no one dared advance on me.

Eventually, he would always grow tired of his sex toys and discard them for good, but he was a legacy and ruled the East Coast. When I had his attention, he gave me his full attention. I was a queen, and he was my king, and I was placed high on a pedestal. Wherever we went, the red carpet rolled out, and I was so proud that people thought of me as his young girlfriend.

My family would always ask me to invite Ed to our family gatherings but knew he would never accept their offers, but he surprised us all one Christmas Eve. I thought he was charming and a complete gentleman that evening, and he was very attentive to me. They tried to accept him, but no one seemed to warm up to him. Ed felt utterly out of his element; he was no king there, and he could not win the female population present there with his sex appeal, so he did not know what to do with himself. He tried for me, but it just was not possible for him to be a family man. I, being the rebellious teen, was more pleased than disappointed with the outcome. I didn't fit in even if I was their flesh and blood.

I never invited him to another occasion, and he never asked to come. He would never come to the door to pick me up either. When we were going out, he sometimes would only honk the horn of his sky-blue Cadillac with the white vinyl hardtop from the driveway; sometimes he did not even pull in the driveway but would block the way waiting for me to run out and jump into the passenger side.

I broke curfew and the rules of the house so many times that my parents finally told me in anger to get out, not thinking I would really do it. Guess what I did? I got an apartment with friends and had three different jobs to make ends meet. I worked as a bartender a few nights at a private club, the Motor Vehicle Department Monday to Friday, and I also worked for Dunkin Donuts, getting up at five each morning to make the donuts on the weekends.

This on-and-off relationship and heartbreak with Ed took a toll. I was as addicted to him as he had been to me, and eventually, he said, "I have been seeing Doctor Stevens. This relationship is so unhealthy for both of us, and he says I have to let you go. 'Go away, run as fast as you can, and be happy.'"

I was free of Ed's allure for many years; he let me go when he met a young woman who was an airline attendant on a trip to Florida. They moved and lived in Florida, and that was where he stayed for many years.

This was the time I connected with my first husband. We were attracted to one another because he was a musician, a perfect one. His father had many published piano recordings and taught him music at a very young age. He could pick up almost any instrument and play it. He was able to read music, unlike me at the time, and could walk into a department store and tell you what key the overhead lights were buzzing. He had perfect pitch.

I had no idea at the time that I was dealing with a very insecure man who won me over with lies and scams. I thought the relationship was healthy. No one had ever loved me like that before; he would be by my side 24/7, and I mistook that attentiveness as unconditional love. However, it was in no way a healthy relationship. What I thought was love was really the actions at the time of a man who would end up being very abusive emotionally and physically to me. I am sure I was not wholly innocent in provoking this behavior as I did have that effect on people it seemed.

I knew what was going on with him during this time—it was all written down in a fifty-page letter written to the Catholic Church Council requesting the annulment of our marriage. I did not care about the church recognizing my legal divorce, which I stated in the letter of explanation to them. The dissolution was something that was so very important to my mother. She had given me so much that I felt that if it was so important to her, it was the least I could give back to her. Besides, it was therapeutic to write it all down, make sense out of it, put it into words, and let it go. This whole part of my life's memories was pretty much gone, but because it was all written down in such detail, I knew the entire story step by step without having to remember or relive the pain. In one paragraph, I wrote, "I don't care if you annul my marriage or not. All the things written are accurate, and God knows that I had just reason to leave, and I tried everything to make it work, and sometimes it just doesn't. I do not need your blessing to end this marriage legally or spiritually. I'm not going to be judged by you or anybody else. This letter of explanation will stay with me."

Before the marriage dissolved, we spent many sessions in marriage counseling with many different counselors. When he did not like what the counselor had to say, he would suggest they were incompetent and give me several examples. His reasons made perfect sense to me at the time, so we would go to another counselor. It was always the same result; they would tell me privately, and try to say to him in a nonthreatening way, that he needed a psychologist and not a marriage counselor. They said that marriage counselors were not equipped to deliver the type of help my husband required, and I should seek professional advice for him.

When we were living together before I agreed to marry him, our relationship was intense. He was off the charts as far as intelligence went. He was so smart that he, unknown to me, had a hard time understanding so-called ordinary people. He felt for some reason to fit in, he had to tell lies and stories. He was smart enough to figure out what people wanted, and he became that person for each of his acquaintances. He would change personalities like he had a dissociative disorder, and he kept all his different characters straight.

His mother knew and tried several times to warn me that her son lived in a false world he made up and to keep my eyes and ears open. She felt I was the best thing for him because I was sincere, reliable, and he adored me enough that maybe, just maybe, he would seek help to conquer his childhood demons so that he could stay with me. I was a little confused about what she was trying to tell me and why she would try to protect me rather than her son. I did not heed her warnings, and we moved in together and got married.

We rented a little house on the coast of Connecticut. It was more like a cottage than a house. It had been moved to its present site from another area and placed behind the homeowner's private residence. The original part of the house was well over a hundred years old. The price was right, oddly very affordable, and we loved it. I immediately felt drawn to its tilted floors and uneven walls and cracked ceilings. It had personality, and it was ours.

I do not know what occurred first—the strange happenings in the house or his weird, bizarre behavior. One night, we were seated in the living room, one of the two places that had been added to the house after it had been moved to its new location. We heard strange music and chanting, starting soft and muffled and slowly getting louder and louder until it became quite annoying. He would yell and scream, "Shut up!"

But the noise continued. I asked the chanting to stop because they or it was scaring me, and it ended as quickly as it started.

Our friends would come out to the house out of curiosity concerning the noises we would tell them about. Some would never hear a thing; the rest would seldom return after having the experience. I tried so hard to understand what the voices were saying, but all I was able to decipher were a few sentences. The dialogue speeded up so fast that the human ear was not able to pick up the words. I recorded the sounds and then played them back at a slow speed. This is what was said: "Go away. You're not going to be here. Go from him. We need you. He needs to go."

I worked as a retailer at the time for a small family-owned department store downtown, and my husband worked for a well-known distributor. We had a different work schedule, so he would have scheduled times of the day in which he would phone me from home and check in. These calls continued until they could no longer get through. He wouldn't be able to call me at home because every time he tried, there was white noise. It would be so bad that I wouldn't be able to hear him on the other side. He could hang up, and someone like my sister or mom would call, and the phone lines were open. I figured someone was playing a terrible joke on us and went to the landlord with a thousand questions about the house and its history.

The landlord just looked at me with no explanation as I played him the recording and talked about all the other strange banging throughout the house, the doors opening and closing by themselves and toilets flushing and bathtubs filling with water when no one had run a bath. Either the landlord knew something he was not willing to share or just thought we were two young adults who were experimenting with drugs or we were just looking for a way out of our lease.

One night while sleeping, I woke up with someone or something pinning me down on the bed; you could see the hand imprint on my wrist that turned white from the pressure of restraints. I could not speak or move, but it was a strange experience, and I was not afraid. I felt myself rise and float to the ceiling—not my body, mind you, just the consciousness of my body. I could feel the stucco ceiling on my cheek. It was rough and cold, and I could see myself as my body rolled over, floating above me, still lying pinned to the bed.

My husband was not in bed next to me as he should be but was crouched in the corner of the room like a frightened child breathing loud and heavy with tears streaming down his face. He was oblivious to my presence, and I could hear the chanting; it was clear then as though I was now vibrating on the same level. The voices were allowing me to listen to their words without a slowed-down recording device. The sounds were directed toward him. "GO AWAY! You're not going to be here. SHE BELONGS TO US. LEAVE HER."

His face was slammed side to side with echoing strokes, and his body was repeatedly lifted and slammed onto the wooden floor. I had no emotional response to this abuse; down deep, I knew he had been deceiving me, and my well-being was in danger. I was just kind of disconnected from the violence he was receiving, void of any concern, and I quickly found myself in the house but at a different time. The house was starkly furnished with items of necessity only. Lightly dimmed lanterns hung in the hallway, casting shadows onto the walls and what appeared to be an entrance and sitting den. There were musical instruments set up as if a party was about to start, and slowly visions of people began to materialize, becoming substantial enough for one to touch. They were all dressed as if it was the 1700s. No one noticed me at first. Then one woman looked straight at me and let out a moan of agony that pierced my ears. They all seemed to see me and aware of my presence then. Their arms were outstretched, grabbing for me, suffocating me. I could not breathe; they were inside me, tearing at me and taking a piece of life from me, all crying in ecstasy as if I was a cold glass of water saving them from the desert heat. I found a voice within myself and screamed from my soul, "LEAVE ME ALONE. LET ME GO!"

I was back in my body, released from my restraints, and my husband remained in the corner in a state of complete and utter shock.

After this experience, we moved out of the house, explaining to the landlord that there was nothing he could do to us that would be worse than what the house was doing to us. He listened to what we were willing to tell him and said nothing except, "I don't believe it is the house. I think it is you" and let us out of the lease and was relieved to see us pack up and go.

Believing and trying to make me concerned once more that I was a witch or possessed, my husband said the other side was always biting at my heels. He would remind me every day, pointing out all the strange phenomena that happened while I was around mainly against him. He was making me feel bad that I and I alone were responsible for the beating that he had received in our house that day.

His manipulations and paranoia had turned into constant stalking. In the beginning, I had no idea that he was the one who followed me. He was trying to instill fear, so I'd be afraid to leave the house or go anywhere without him. It had gotten so bad that I considered police involvement at one point for the mind games he was playing, the mental and physical abuse—all of which occurred when I was seven months pregnant with his child. He would manipulate people into believing I did things that were the farthest from the truth as truth could be, and he made sure that I had no friends to give me support, no car to go anywhere, no job to be independent. He slowly broke me down. I believed that I absolutely needed him, and I was afraid to leave.

I was so frightened and thought he would take my child from me and then have me killed. I was an abused wife and mother, and no one knew.

He did this over time. He did this with twisted mind games and isolation and turned me into a shell of myself. My family finally started to pick up inconsistencies in the stories and incidents and they began to see the occasional bruise on an arm or leg when he made the mistake of not aiming right to hide his violent nature. Most of the abuse was mental anyway, and who sees that? I believe psychological abuse is worse sometimes.

My brother-in-law was the first to take my side and investigate the lies that he started to pick up on while playing his weekly game of golf with him, knowing I was home yet again with my daughter day after day and week after week.

When he was confronted by my family and once I knew I had their support and they no longer believed that I was crazy evil or unfit as a mother, he repented and begged for forgiveness and promised to seek help. We were recommended to Doctor Stevens. I did not at the time put it together that this doctor might be the same one that told Ed he had to let me go. If he was, he never let on. He was not nearby. We had to travel a good forty-five minutes away by car, but we went weekly and then twice a week for a while. We had sessions together and sessions separate from one another, and then the doctor told him that he did not need to see me any longer, but he required that my husband continue his visits alone. He did continue under great protest, but life just got worse because all his lies had come full circle and he had to face them.

The doctor called me into the office one day and told me to go home, pack up my daughter, and leave. I was to go to my parents or anywhere, but I had to leave immediately. He said that my husband was a walking time bomb ready to explode, and I was his target, and the doctor was worried about our safety.

I thank the universe every day for bringing me to Doctor Stevens. He was the first one to recognize the real truth of what I was living. He was the first person to see through the brilliance of my husband's mind and see what he was capable of doing. I never lied to Doctor Stevens about the experiences I had with the paranormal. I told him everything so that if he thought I was certifiable, he would let me know. He helped me find my dignity and helped me rediscover my fighting instincts. I did not know at the time that this was not the last time I would hear Doctor Stevens's name. God help any other person who tries to hurt my daughter or me ever again. The guns and protective self-survival instincts, I had them all. "What doesn't kill you will make you stronger" was never as accurate as in my case. My husband knew he had lost. One of the last statements I made to him before our legal divorce was, "Do not ever underestimate me again."

I raised my daughter by myself for many years with the help of my family. I realized my family was my lifeline; they loved me and wanted to protect their own.

Tabitha and I had our home. I had a great job and made an excellent living even though I did not have a college degree. I dated but never got serious with anyone. I was independent and intended to stay that way—plus, no one man seemed to be able to hold ground with me. I cursed Ed many times for ruining sex for me with anyone else—maybe for the rest of my life—and thus allowed him back into my life from time to time for my occasional needed fix. Ed knew that was all it was at that point and accepted it. We would always have a bond, and we kind of understood each other and took one another for who and what we were, which was not precisely clear.

Chapter 6

The Other Side

Everything was going grand in a very healthy way if there is such a thing until that day the accident occurred and then things started full circle again. The year was 1989. I know because I wrote it all down. After coming back from the other side of the death experience, I had a sense of peace about me. I was no longer afraid of death, just the process of it. I had seen the other side, and I welcomed it when it was my time.

Since I wanted to know, I had looked into the future. Since I had asked to see, I received the gift of sight. I healed physically because of my request that I will be well, and because I asked to be secure and not afraid of the unknown, I received the power to be alone. I was given information about my own past life so I would know that the details shown to me in the future were indeed accurate, and I would recognize them when it was time to act, and there would be no doubt. I'd get healed. I'd find my place in the human race. I would meet my life partner who needed me as much as I needed him within seven days of my rebirth. He would be the earthbound anchor that enables me. I would move to a learning place where I would continue to get healthy. I would find my human life, and I would travel in a world filled with adventure and knowledge of the kind that is of importance. I had to push myself away from the familiar and comfortable.

I was being shown a familiar place with familiar terrain. I could smell honeysuckles, and I felt like I was coming home. I saw these places in my childhood dream, flying over the rolling hills of green pastures and the forest and gliding down into a white farmhouse, a small long field with a vast body of water at the rear of the area. Beyond that, there was a line of evergreens. The energy was calling me home, holding me close. Okay, I knew I would be there someday.

I also embraced other predictions—that I would work among the children, that soon, only seven significant banks would exist, and there would be one world currency. The New World Order would ring throughout the land. It would start with bar codes on everything we purchase—eventually, bar codes and electronic chips placed under our skin. The governments will know where we live, what we buy, and how much. No cash would be exchanged. Governments would control every aspect of our lives, and we would accept it because of fear and the false sense of security governments offer.

The planet as we know it would come to an end when pandemics kill much of the population. Citizens would not be allowed to move outside their nation or region unless they own land somewhere because of the possibility of crime, war, and natural disasters that throw off the equilibrium of the planet. Food would be unavailable, and overpopulation in more desirable areas would create social strife, political hatred, and total anarchy. Beware of the man in the blue turban who stands next to the leader of the free world for he is the last Antichrist.

The West Coast of America would fall into the ocean, and the middle of the country will suffer floods and earthquakes as many other places far and near will experience wild and strange nature. Where winters are cold, they will get colder. Where summers are hot, they will get warmer. The East Coast would have nuclear fallout, and a chain reaction would occur, destroying New York City. There would be a hurricane and flashflood on the west coast of Florida from an ocean quake, devouring much of the state and leaving the rest with no drinking water. Rising waters would destroy towns and beach residences. Sun flares would come down from the heavens, destroying what is left on this earth—there would be no source of food, drinkable water, shelter, or sanity. People would be desperate to survive and keep their families alive, willing to kill or be killed.

Members of particular nations are well aware of these consequences, and the wealthy people of the world have invested, prepared to hit the brink. Most of us do not have the means to do so, nor have we been told what to do. The wealthy and powerful paid for shelters to protect them. They have been sworn to secrecy by the pledge of salvation for their families and feel that they are justified in their acts and blessed because only the strong and powerful can succeed and survive and they are the ones chosen to continue. The rest of the country—yeah, there's no time.

My last job on this earth is to live, learn, teach, and enlighten all who ask, to help others to be prepared as much as possible. I could do this only if I stayed alive, which meant I had to write it down to help them believe. I had to leave my current comfortable life, start my adventures, and find my place. Is this the price to pay for my gift back to health, back to my daughter, to experience the gift of unconditional love, to know the truth?

I will reside in a faraway land where I will find the peace. I will need to write it all down so that I can teach all who want to know and will listen.

So far, almost all the information given to me has transpired or is transpiring as I continue to write it down.

Chapter 7

I'm Here: The Seventh Day of My Rebirth

I was sitting in my studio cell when the phone rang. It was my mother. "I want you to get dressed and walk down to that little Seaside Tavern right down the street, have a glass of soda, and see people. Get back out there. Talk to people. Live again! Then come home and call me. You know that it is time and that you have to do this, so why procrastinate any further? Just do it."

I had been thinking about doing just that anyway, and her call confirmed it and pushed me enough to get up and get dressed. I felt so lost and so insecure. *What do I even wear? I look awful. If I know people and do not recognize them, how will they react to that?*

What a child I was being. With everything I knew at that point and all the crap I had lived through, how bad could this be? I just had to get dressed and do it. I walked down the wooden back staircase of my little studio apartment, which seemed too short, and across the back parking lot with its cracked black asphalt into the side street where I could see the little Seaside Tavern, which was my destination.

It was summer and very bright outside, so as soon as I entered the historic building that rested on the shoulder of the New England Sound, it was hard to adjust my eyes to see my way through the next door into the tavern. My ears started to ring, and my vision dimmed. My arms and legs began to tingle, and I thought I would faint any minute and wanted to cry out and run away from all the outlines of people who sat in the tall stools at the bar or ate lunch at the surrounding varnished-top tables.

I was trying to run back to my sanctuary. Still, I couldn't move. I had tunnel vision and couldn't see anything or anyone except one person at the end of the tunnel. He was moving closer and closer to my space: familiar blue eyes, his dark skin, blond hair, and a quiet, inviting, soothing voice. "Hey, there, Augusta, are you all right? You look white as a ghost."

My nightmare became a reality. *Oh, no! He knows me, and I do not remember him.* I told myself not to panic. *You can get through this. Just act natural and explain later when the time is better.*

He took my hand and led me to an empty stool at the bar and stood there next to me, very close, with his hand attached to mine, his shoulder touching mine in an attempt to help me balance so that I would not succumb to the fainting path I was heading down. His name was Luke—I definitely knew him

I calmed down as we talked for quite a while, and I started to believe that everything was going to be all right again. Without reservation, I invited Luke back to my little apartment a block away to continue our conversation away from the sounds of the barflies around us. I could call my mother again and reassure her that I was all right and not catch her in total distress at my doorstep.

It was time to exit the tavern anyway. I started to feel eyes on me. I wondered how many of them I knew. I struggled with this possibility. The town was small, and everyone knew someone who knew someone else. Alternatively, I wondered if they had heard of my misfortune and loss of memory and pondered if they should approach me. I wanted to tell my knight in shining armor of my situation, but why be so dramatic and possibly set me up as a babbling, mentally and physically disabled nutcase before he even got to know me at all? So I stayed away from the subject altogether. Instead, we talked about life in general and our mutual viewpoints on different topics as we walked to my place, and I called my mother, leaving out the part that I had company.

We talked for hours that day, and I knew so far I was relieved that he had not yet started down the memory-lane road. I knew it was inevitable, and so it was. "So what is your story?" he asked. "There is something that I just can't put my finger on. I have known you on and off for years, yet you seem different somehow."

Okay, this was my window of opportunity to start explaining very gently so as not to freak him out completely. "I know that you know me, and I am sorry—I should have said something long before now, but I had an accident a while ago, and I have lost much of my memory and the people there. I do not remember you from the past—only today. I would like to get to know you again if you're up for a challenge."

There was a blank look on his face followed by a smile and almost a bit of relief. "Oh well, that explains a lot. I feel so much better now."

I could not tell if he was being sarcastic, had a dry sense of humor, or if he was sincere. He went over our past general encounters, and I was trying desperately to put the pieces together. I did remember, kind of, like flashes of images along with stories my sister told me I had related to her. *Oh my god, I had slept with him! How embarrassing. My sister told me I said I was very disillusioned and lacked interest in pursuing him after our little frolic in the hay. Bummer, this must be that guy. Now what do I do?*

I decided that whatever attracted me to him way back then as a teenager must still be there, and now that I was kind of a different person, maybe things could be different. Then I remembered he was married and had a couple of kids. *That is just great—the first guy I invite back to my house is someone I should just have had a friendly conversation with and left at the bar. I guess I have to learn how to read people better.*

"How come you have not mentioned all this time that you are married? What's your story?" I asked in a condescending tone. "You seem to have left that part out."

He told me he was indeed married and had children. Luke was a nineteen-year-old boy in the navy when he met his wife. She was then a sexy twenty-five-year-old and, at the time, seemed like just want he wanted. He found himself with a child every time he would return home on shore leave and had three by the time he got out of the service. He tried to make the marriage work. His children were the most crucial thing in his life, and in a last-ditch effort, he moved them all down to Florida where his wife insisted they go.

Luke was now legally separated from her though the marriage had been emotionally and physically over for years. He remained in the same house, not wanting to leave the children with a broken parent—his wife. Luke lived his own life and financially supported them, and as long as Luke stayed with them and paid the bills, his wife closed her eyes to his many years of womanizing and his separate secret life. When he agreed to move away from his familiar stomping grounds, he was lost and realized how genuinely miserable life had become. There was nothing worse than not caring about anything every morning when he woke up except his kids, so he returned to his childhood home of thirty-plus years and was looking for a job and a new place to live.

Luke stayed with his mother and father for a while to get his head straight, so he could bring his children back to be with him. He had only been back in town for seven days. I thought to myself, *He came back the day that I died and was reborn.*

LB

I don't know when I put together that his initials were *LB*, the same initials of the prediction I made that day with the tarot cards because the last thing I planned on was to get too involved with a man who was still married but said he was finally leaving his wife of twenty years. He had no legal income, lived with his mommy and daddy, and had three kids, no legitimate work, and a reputation with the ladies. He was seeing a doctor that was helping him through his own PTSD issue, and I was shocked to learn his name was Dr. Stevens, who kept in touch with me from time to time just check in. I knew now that Dr. Stevens had to connect the dots. I found it interesting that the three men in my life at some point were keeping company with this doctor. I never understood precisely why this Doctor Stevens kept showing up in my life other than the doctor was there to help me.

The fact of the matter was I had nothing either. At least Luke had his health, and he was working on his problems, and the doc did not tell him he should leave me. I did not have my health or a job, no real friends who I remembered, and no car—heck, I also did not have a memory. Who was I to judge him or anyone else? *Everybody deserves a second chance,* I reminded myself. As long as I was smart about it, he could still be one of my first new friends. I did not have to and was not going to get romantically involved with him. I went that route one time before with him anyway and was disappointed.

We hung out, and he met my daughter who seemed to tolerate him but kept her distance, being afraid to let a man get too close. We met each other's families who unexpectedly opened their doors to each of us with almost a sigh of gratitude that we spent time together. My family knew he was going through a divorce and was still legally married with kids, but they did not seem too worried about it. Plus I reassured them we were just good friends and had no romantic involvement. I do not even think they would have cared that much if we were involved that way. It made me think about how bad I was and what kind of heartache I had given them in my former life. Was I a female hound dog? Did they find him to be the right person for me because he also was a hound dog? His family seemed to love me and wanted me to come to all their family events and went out of their way to make me comfortable. The truth of the matter was I did want to take the relationship to the next level; he was just so damn good to me and never once made a possible unwanted advance toward me. He was so patient with my recovery—mental and physical—and was just happy to spend time with me.

I wanted to bring up the subject of those first encounters that I kind of remembered, the holes that were filled in by my sister, so I said one day, "Do you remember Jerry, the bartender at the members-only club?"

"Oh, sure I do. I have known Jerry for years. He wasn't pleased, I think back then, with me getting involved with you.

"I believe he was jealous of you, Luke, and a little protective. I hear that he's down somewhere in Florida."

"Why would he be jealous? I only brought you a few drinks that night and gave you a ride home on my motorcycle when Ed did not show up to get you. I was a little in love with you though or attracted anyway. I will admit that. You were so cute, strumming your guitar and singing up there. I remember thinking how brave you must be to be able to do that in front of all those people, and your songs were original and had a soul. I had to kiss you that night. Do you remember any of that?"

"Strangely enough, I do. It must have meant something to me because I do remember. I wanted to see you again and kept looking for you to return to the club. When you came back in that night and you sang a few of your songs, I decided that I wanted to see you again, so that is why I met you at the Roadside Inn."

"What? What are you saying? I never saw you for a second time like that? I don't play guitar or sing. The next time was when Ed left you stranded again, and you needed a ride home and another night when Ed thought he was introducing us for the first time at the Cross Street Café. You asked me if we had met before, and I said probably in another life, and I assumed you did not want Ed to know we had spent any time together, and I left it at that. Other than that, I would see you around town, but we never talked, and you completely ignored me, so I just left you alone, seeing that I was married anyway, and Jerry told me to stay away from you because Ed was known to be very possessive of you. I did not need that in my life. I think your memories are a little mixed up. That was not me. I don't play guitar and certainly have never performed on stage. I am involved in music only because I like it, and my side profession allowed me to connect to rock bands like Mountain, Peter Frampton, the Band, and a few others."

"There is a guy I know, not well, but his name is Luke also, and he kind of looks likes me, and he is an entertainer, and I know he occasionally plays in the area. I believe he moved his family to California. Did you think he was me and you, you what? What did you do? Never mind, I don't want to know."

Oh my god! That is what Jerry must have meant when he said to me, "He is not who you think he is." That is why I did not feel the same connection with him. Not the same Luke yet another who understandably was a disappointment that night. Wow, if this is a taste of life's confusion to come, I am going to have a wild ride.

Chapter 8

The Move

Luke said, "Let's move away from here. I want to bring you and your daughter to Florida with me. You have nothing keeping you here. Life will be more comfortable for you in a new place. You have a unique experience, so why not a new beginning in a new location?"

He was right. It was so tricky running into people that I did not remember, and you just could not stop and tell everyone your story, and I did not even know if I should be telling them. How well did I know them in the past anyway? Could I trust them not to laugh at me or think I was some kind of freak? Moving to a place where no one knew me and I know I did not know them would be the best thing to do, so we packed up the few belongings we had. We drove down to the east coast of Florida with a twelve-year-old car, a few household items, and $500 in our pocket.

He promised he would take care of us no matter what, and I believed him. He was terrific with my daughter, and she trusted him although at eight years old, she had a look that would scare even the most assured man. She still did not believe, and like her mother, she was stubborn and self-reliant. She had become accustomed to taking care of me and told Luke many times, "I can take care of her you know. We don't need you. We are coming with you because we want to go. We are not coming for any other reason."

Any grown adult would step back when a statement like that comes out of an eight-year-old.

He was worried about finding a place to live with no security deposit or the last month's rent as most landlords required. I believe his mother helped him out with that although he never told me that for sure. I felt awful because I still was not able to hold down a job to help him, and he never pressured me about it or made me feel like a burden to him. I was still weak with muscle spasms that would make it too difficult to work through a full day.

I had a hard time reading—did not remember the words. Math, in general, was the most difficult. I had the basic concept down, but I just could not put it all together fast enough to even work in a grocery checkout line. The worst thing was that my words would come out all jumbled. I would know what I wanted to say and just use words that were close but not quite right. Luke would smile and correct me and said it was so cute. I did not think so. I was embarrassed and afraid I was going to make a fool of myself in front of people who would think I was an uneducated idiot. I guess, at this point, I was illiterate, but I was not an idiot. The history, geography, the music I once loved and knew how to read and write, experiences both good and bad, for the most part, gone. Spelling, well, that goes without saying. I did not know the spelling. How does one find a job and function in a world that is so unforgiving?

I trusted in Luke and myself though. I was supposed to continue, and if all the future insight I was given was even half right, it was all going to be okay. I just had to go with the flow and believe it would all work out. I might not know the past as other people did, but I knew the future and other essential things that other people did not. I thought that was a fair tradeoff.

We rented a great little house in a typical Florida neighborhood where all the houses looked the same except for color. The lawns were mowed, the kids played in the street until dark, and barbeque block parties were a weekly event. Luke held down two jobs to make ends meet, and I kept house trying to learn and reeducate myself. My daughter went to school every day and would ask Luke to help her with her homework, knowing that I could not. She was adjusting to Florida's life, and Luke was happy to be with us and near his children who now lived about five miles away. They did not like me very much and thought I was to blame for their father and mother being apart. They had no idea that I was just the one who finally pulled him away, but I was not the one who kept him out all hours of the night when they were growing up. He had his night job and other jobs that kept him busy. They had to blame someone, so the blame fell on me. For many years, they made my life a living hell.

In our suburban neighborhood, I befriended a woman named Carol. Carol was one of the few at that time who knew my story, and she was a professor at the community college in the next town over. She came to me one day and asked if I was ready to go to work; she had a proposal for me, and if I had the guts, she had the means. Carol told me she hoped I was not mad at her, but she had spoken with an administrator at the college about me and my situation, and they had an idea if I was up for it. The college offered me a job in the Center for Leadership Development (CPI) lab from 8:00 AM to 12:00 PM as a greeter. I would sign books in and out of the library to students who needed them. After my shift, from 1:00 PM to 4:00 PM, the professors in the lab all agreed to reeducate me academically.

The CPI Lab was a library. Professors worked a few hours a day to help students who needed to get up to speed, pass the test, and earn credits that would allow them to move to different colleges of their choice. Most of them had to complete programs that they had not yet mastered, and there were various methods and extra help in the lab to accomplish this.

Many of the teachers were younger than me, and many were around my age; in time, they all knew and understood why I was there, and I believe that they were the most helpful people I have ever met. A true educator would feel very excited and most likely reminded of the profound reason they had chosen teaching as a profession. For a teacher to make a difference in someone's life is the ultimate achievement and satisfaction for them—to educate someone who wants to learn and will hold on to and cherish every word these teachers had to say. For them, I was that person.

I was like a sponge, and I could not learn enough or fast enough. I would read every book given to me—from the simplest to eventually very complicated deep, mind-altering literature. I was so happy and no longer felt inadequate and afraid that people would not accept me. I had a whole lot of new friends. It took me a little over two years to work my way to a level considered to be equivalent to two years of college.

I would probably still be there learning, but it was time to move to the west coast where Luke had a job opportunity that would pay a lot more money and he would be able to have just one job, and not many, to make ends meet. We had friends there, believe it or not. It was Jerry who had moved to the west coast of Florida years before, and he was well connected in the construction world. Jerry was the one who found this new position and offered it to Luke. We lived just around the corner from him and his wife of ten years.

Luke did not push me to find work right away, but I forced myself. I needed to carry my weight and be more independent. He was my best friend, but he had also become overprotective of me and very much like a father. I was feeling like a rebellious teenager. I wanted to live and have fun and have my own money so that I did not have to ask for money every time I wanted something. He never denied me anything. If I genuinely wanted it, he would find a way of getting it for me, but it was not the same as getting it on my own. He had to start letting go and let me make my own mistakes. It was time for him to trust me enough to know that I was more potent than before, and just because I was coming full circle didn't mean that I wouldn't need or love him any less. The difference would be that I was with him not because I needed to be but because I wanted to be. I realized my daughter said that once. I could even learn something from the mouths of babes.

He kept asking to make an honest woman of me and marry him, but I kept avoiding the subject. "Luke, I know we have been together for a while now, but I have not healed completely, and I still do not know me, who I am, and I seem to be changing every day. We disagree a lot more these days—not fighting because I can't get you to fight with me—but maybe when I finally become me again or change too much, you might find out you don't like me very much. I keep learning and searching, and everything is so exciting and unusual to me. You look at the world differently than I do. You love to take care of me and protect me, and I don't want a father—I want to be free. We can't have any babies together even if I was younger because the accident made that impossible. Plus, I am happy with just Tabitha, and you already have three children of your own, so why get married? Marriage is if you want to have a family. Why can't we just leave things the way they are? We are all good, right?"

I knew I could hold him off for a while but could see it was a very sore subject, and it meant a lot to Luke for me to agree to a forever commitment with him. Kidding around trying to give me more time, I made Luke a proposition. "Tell you what, Luke, you know how much I want to have a horse, right? I have been reading a lot about how they help people who have muscle problems, and riding and being with a horse is like the best therapy. You buy me a horse so that I can ride, and I will marry you."

I laughed and gave him a big kiss on the lips, thinking I was okay for a while when he said," Funny you should say that. I have a house I want you to see in the Estates, and it could be set up for horses real easy. It would be a stretch to pay the mortgage with only one salary coming in, but would you like to see it?"

"You are kidding me, right? Really, yeah, let's see it now. I guess we are getting married."

Chapter 9

Florida Life and the Face of Death

Entering the kitchen, I said to Luke, "It's time to get a real job anyway. Tabitha is old enough now to walk to the bus stop in the morning for school. She is old enough now to come home and be on her own, or maybe I can find a job that allows me to be back by three. There are plenty of neighbors here who have kids of their own who will probably be in Tabitha's class and would be willing to keep an eye on her also. What do you think?"

Luke said, "If you think you are ready, Augusta, and it is what you want to do, then sure! It would help out our financial situation here. They are giving me a company truck to use, so you can have the car. Have you thought about what you want to do?"

"Gosh no, I haven't a clue. I will pick up a paper tomorrow and start looking to see what is out there. Maybe a clothing store. I did that once, right? How about selling cars again? They said I was good at that. I can't imagine doing that or that I ever did. I think I will stay away from that profession this time around. I don't like children enough to run after them all day, and even though there are a million older people here that need nursing, I would hate that. I am used to being nursed, not to being the nurse, and I don't have that kind of patience or nurturing in me. Stop laughing at me. I know it is true. You don't have to tell me."

The *Naples Daily News* was tiny compared with *The Norwalk Hour* in Connecticut—half the size and only one page of classified ads. I knew this was not going to be easy, but I read that newspaper every day and laughed every time I came to headlines: "DOG RUNS INTO THE STREET AND ALMOST

CAUSES A TWO-CAR CRASH," "MAN FOUND SLEEPING IN THE PARK COVERED UP WITH THE 'DO NOT SLEEP IN PARK' SIGN." Oh, boy, Luke had moved them to Mayberry!

Luke lovingly and sincerely reminded me that I might be better off finding a job that did not demand for me to be on my feet. I was 100 percent better than in the years before but still had those occasional spasms and asthma attacks when I got tired or ran into something new in the air. My body could not handle these situations since those awful steroids robbed me of the ability and the means to fight impurities in the air. Sometimes the pain made it difficult to complete a task. That's what he was afraid of, and he didn't want me to get a job and be crushed if I couldn't do it.

Although I was appreciative of Luke's concerns, I knew this was one of the reasons I had to get out there and at least try. He would never let go and was over-the-top protective, and I needed to be independent and push forward. I could do it—hell, I would do it. I had to make him understand who I was or who I thought I could be.

With the sun hours away from rising, I woke up as if the house was on fire; I had a familiar heartbeat that I not only felt in my chest but also was virtually visible pumping under my skin. I would always get freaked out when it happened; when it did, it meant something was going to happen that was going to play a big part in my life. I wondered what it would be this time. I had to wait to find out, but I knew it was going to be the day that I found a job because this was the one thing I had been fixated on for more than two weeks and it was important to me. I could think of nothing else; I was almost obsessed with it. Even though this was my first thought, the doubt was still there that that conclusion could have been wrong because sometimes I would presume things only to find out I was entirely out of the ballpark.

The advertisement read, "Assistant needed to General Manager of the Golf and Country Club. Apply in person. The applicant must have organizational skills." *Okay, I can organize it.* "Must be able to type and know WordPerfect and DOS." *Well, I knew WordPerfect, but what is DOS?* "General office skills required as well as robust phone-answering, with people skills a must." *Perfect except for this DOS thing.* "Apply in person."

Was 8:00 AM too early to arrive? Maybe 9:00 AM would be better. I wondered how many others would be there applying for the same position. *What can I do to stand out? Why would he hire me and not someone else with better qualifications. What should I wear? What do I say, and how much does it pay? Can I handle this? I feel sick.*

I started to panic and was just about ready to throw in the towel when I felt a reassuring hand on my shoulder; a calmness came over me, and a smile or confidence surrounded me. I smelled flowers, honeysuckle? A familiar friend was there. I thought to myself, *Thank God nobody else can hear my thoughts because they would put me away.* I knew I could not talk about certain subjects and beliefs because most of the people in the world would tag me as an out-there freak and tell their children to stay away from the strange lady down the street.

I decided to compromise and arrive at 8:30 AM. I put on one of the only skirts and fancy blouses I had. It was on the short side, a kind of silky material, an evergreen color with red flowers, and a matching shirt. My shoes were maroon platform heels. *This outfit is a little young for me,* I thought. *A person of my age should be wearing a more conservative dress with flats or at least pump shoes. Well, it is too late to worry about it now even if it is not an appropriate interview outfit because it will have to do.*

Luke had offered me money to go out and buy something new a week ago, and I was sorry that I did not take him up on his offer then. *Too late now, this would have to do.*

I knew things didn't always just happen. I needed to encourage them to make it work. I knew when it came to something that might be in my cards, no matter what I did or didn't do or attempted to change the course, it wouldn't make any difference. I had the free will to choose how to get there. The outcome would be what I decided.

If this job were an essential part of my future journey, it would be; if not, I would look ahead to my next choice. As long as I at least tried and was true to myself, anything was possible. I decided I was just as good as anyone else and deserved this job as much as any other person who might be there to snatch it up.

There were two other people already there with résumés in hand. In their early twenties, I guessed. I did not have a résumé, and it did not even occur to me that I might need one. What would I put on a résumé anyway?

Education: 2 years. *Oh yeah, that will go over big,* I giggled to myself.

Job history: I don't know in reality, but I was a waitress, a bartender, a front desk clerk at the Motor Vehicle office, a car salesperson at two different dealerships.

Skills: I would put down all the requirements they asked for except for that DOS thing.

Interests: Horses, learning, and traveling

Accomplishments: Surviving, I did that well. No one else cared about that except my family, and I did have two articles about me in *Working Mothers Magazine* and *Working Women* for being one of the first women to sell cars. The magazines were written back when I was in my midtwenties, and seeing a woman selling cars was a real surprise back then; not only did I sell them but I also excelled at selling them, running circles around the guys. That still blows my mind when I think of myself selling vehicles and trucks and reading those published articles. I did have those articles with me. My mother was very proud of my accomplishments and kept those articles in her scrapbook, sharing them with her breakfast ladies' club that met every Saturday morning back home.

I filled out the application in place of a résumé, and when it came to the part of the salary requirement, I put down "Negotiable."

The door at the end of the hallway opened, and an older applicant who was maybe in her fifties came out and exited the front door, and the pretty blonde girl with the long legs went in next. She was not there very long. I did not know if that was a good thing or not. Was she just that perfect, so he did not need to talk to her too long, or was she that bad that he just said thank you for coming and shuffled her out the door?

There was one more to go before me. This applicant had dark brown hair, wore a suit, and looked very professional and qualified. This one concerned me as a possible threat. Compared with her, I felt like a fish out of water.

Ms. Professional was in there for a long time. *He must like her,* I thought. *Oh well, there will be other job interviews. Don't get all depressed because you don't get this one. Breathe. This is the first interview you have been on for years. You are expecting too much from yourself.*

The office door opened once more—this time for me.

"Hi, my name is Nelson, and I am the general manager of the hotel, and you must be Augusta? Please take a seat."

Nelson, not using his last name, like his shiny gold name tag, said. Well, at least he is not stuffy. He had a friendly handshake and warm smile, and I said, "Yes, my name is Augusta." I sat down, and my eyes scanned the office filled with piles of paperwork and clutter. I had never seen such a mess. *How could anyone work in this chaos?* There were piles of files on the desk so high that they were sure to topple over any minute, and every corner of the floor had the same. He smoked, and the ashtray was full of butts, with a cigarette still smoldering in the ashtray just waiting to reignite all the other filter butts. *Chain-smoker, you think, or does he just never empty that thing?*

Without thinking and before I could pull the words back, I said, "Wow, you do need an assistant." I waited for the look of disapproval and disgust on Nelson's face, my prospective boss, and wanted to rewind that first minute of conversation, erasing that last comment, but it was too late; it was already out there. There was a blank look on his face and silence. *Wow, I blew this interview and did it in record time.*

A little smile in the corner of his mouth appeared, followed by a big grin, a snicker, and the full sound of laughter. "Yes, I do, Augusta, but my office is off-limits. It is an organized mess, and I know just where everything is, but I like the fact that you say what is on your mind. You are not from around here, are you? Let me take a look at your résumé."

"Oh, well, I don't have one," I said, "but I did fill out your application form, and I can tell you anything you want to know."

As Nelson began to read the application, he said, "From Connecticut, born and raised! I am too. I grew up in Danbury. Do you know where that is?"

"Yes, one of my sisters lives there now. Where did you live? How long ago did you leave Danbury and arrive here in Florida?"

"I left Danbury about fifteen years ago and started working for the owners of this hotel. Two brothers, they own this hotel and the Wooden Suites down by the Estates. I am the general manager for both properties and need someone to help me keep up with the office work around here. I see that most of your working experience has been in sales and retail but not much office experience. Why do you want this job, and why should I hire you?"

Okay, think quickly, I thought. *This is a critical interview question.* "Well, even though I have not had direct office experience per se, I always had to organize and do all my paperwork in my sales jobs. The only thing the dealerships supplied me with was the cars to sell, a desk, a phone, and the customers. I had to do everything else myself. I did not have an assistant to file my paperwork or calculate the loan payments or process the paperwork with a financial institution. Back when I sold cars, there were no finance managers who did all the necessary paperwork that followed after you sold your customer the car. The salesperson had to do it all. I had to sell the vehicle, take their application for a loan, find a bank that would finance it, make sure the car was ready for them to pick up, and heck, if necessary, I would even have to clean the darn thing. I did whatever was needed to get that car out the door, keep the customer happy, and then make sure they remembered me so they would send their friends to me to buy their next vehicle. So you see, that gave me the office experience you need here. I don't know the hotel business, but it is customer service, right? And I would have to talk to people on the phone every day and accommodate them every day, so my people skills would come in handy, don't you think? Besides, I want the job, and I need the job, and I know you would not be sorry you hired me."

"Why not go back to selling cars? You were very good at it, and it would pay more than what we are offering for a salary here."

I knew why I left the business back then. My family told me that things had changed in the industry. Management companies came in, and the salespeople became puppets. They sold the car, yeah, but they had to play games now with the average customer: "I don't know if I can sell the vehicle to you at that price. Give me a deposit, and I'll go to my boss." From there, the customer was shuffled off to the finance manager who played the next set of games, trying to sell them undercarriage protection and paint protection, life insurance, loan insurance, and the kitchen sink. They even took away the most significant perk of all—the demo cars that the top salespeople got to drive as their own. "No, I do not want to go back. Been there, done that, time to move on."

Before I realized it, an hour had passed. I knew a lot about him, and he knew as much about me as I allowed. We developed a bond.

"Well, Augusta, even though you do not have the exact experience I am looking for, I am going to give you a chance. I like your enthusiasm, and I believe we will work well together. The pay is only $18,000 a year, but we give a cost of living raise every year, and you will have an opportunity to learn as much as you want about the business. If education has value for you, welcome to Florida, and welcome aboard. Let me introduce you to the rest of the staff."

I exited his office, and behind the desk directly outside his office sat a woman with salt-and-pepper hair whom he introduced as the office manager, Helen.

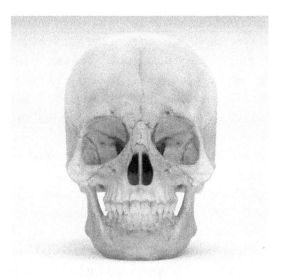

I froze and hoped no one noticed the horror on my face. Helen was going to die soon. I knew this because there was that familiar skeleton vision in her face that I would see when one was close to death. I had not seen that vision for quite some time. The face of death, I called it. I knew it meant Helen's time working with me would be short. I wanted to run up and hug her and tell her not to be frightened because it was not the end but a new beginning. I learned never to say anything because many times, these people had no idea, and unless they knew they were ill and dying and seeking comfort, I would never say a word to them or anyone close to them. I recognized death's face but never knew how the end would come or exactly when, only that it was surely within six months. Helen did not look ill; she had a calmness about her, so she did not know yet that she was sick, or maybe it would be a tragic accident that takes her away.

I snapped back to attention.

"This is Jeff. He is the sales manager here and handles all the group reservations, whether they just have overnight rooms or want a golf package with catering for the groups that want to come. We have a catering manager who handles all our banquets and parties and a front desk manager who handles all the individual reservations, and of course, there is an accounting office. They all work in the building next door. You will be introduced to them all later. Your desk is here. Well, that is it for now. I will have someone show you the golf course when you start on Monday. You can start on Monday, right?"

"Yes, sir!" I shook his hand. "Thank you. Thank you very much! You will not be sorry."

The weekend went fast, and by Monday at 8:00 AM, I sat behind my office desk waiting for my first instructions.

"Good morning, Augusta, you type, right? I need this letter typed up first, and then Helen will show you how to enter these data into the system. We have a DOS program that she will teach you to use. I know you don't know DOS, but no problem. It's easy once you get the hang of it."

During the week, I got to know just about everyone there—from the golf course employees to the dishwasher in the kitchen—and was feeling more and more each day that I belonged.

Luke was thrilled that I had found a job so quickly and seemed happy, and Tabitha had been fortunate in her new place; she had several friends from the neighborhood. Everything was just so natural and beautiful for about four months.

"Good morning, Nelson, where is Helen today?"

"Oh, she called out sick, so I will need you to do some of her work if you don't mind."

"Not at all, I don't mind at all. Just show me what you would like done." I wondered if this was the beginning of death's visit or if she was just sick with a cold or something and there was nothing to worry about other than catching some germs. The face of death only appears the very first time I meet someone; its ugly face never shows on the same person more than once. Why it has to reveal itself to me in the first place was baffling to me. What can I do? Was I supposed to do something? Could I do anything at all? I tried to warn people when I was a young child but found out quickly that people freaked out, and no one wanted to play with a freak. Kids can be cruel, and I was forbidden by my mother ever to speak about the subject again.

I always told Luke everything though he did find it unsettling, and the first few times, he would just laugh it off. He did not question me anymore because if I said someone was going to die, they did. Together, we figured out that if I saw death in a person's face, I should go that extra step to be kind to him/her. I should be there for these folks with a helping hand and an open ear. Hence, if it was an illness that was to take them away and they were seeking comfort, they would feel a pull toward me. I would have the opportunity to tell them of my death experience and the other side and how not to be scared and how peaceful it was, a much better place than the one they were leaving. It helped them, and I shared that with them because they would ask.

If it was a tragic death like a car accident, there was nothing I could do about that except be a good friend to them while they were still here. The gift, if you want to call it that, always came with a price. Sometimes I could help, so the death face had a purpose. Other times, it was just an awful curse with no useful purpose at all but to give me nightmares.

It was a Tuesday in November, and it had been a few weeks since Helen had sat behind her desk. Nelson announced to the rest of the staff that she would not be returning. Diagnosed with fast-growing brain cancer, she was expected to pass in a couple of months. This vision happened very quickly and gave me no time to get close enough to Helen that she might seek comfort from me so that I could help her pass over. Oh, how I hated that face of death. It was cruel and unforgiving.

Travel and See the World

Helen's job position was eliminated. I picked up some of her work, and the rest was spread around for others to complete. Helen's job consisted of more contact with the public and hotel guests as well as hospitality tasks. I seemed to be a natural at this part, but I struggled with the office duties of typing and composing letters and contracts. Spelling was the worst part. It slowed me down so much, and I would not pick up on misspelled words that my boss would find, making notes with red marker on my finished work (I thought) for me to see and retype. He had patience, but I could see in his face that he was losing it at times.

"Augusta, do you have a minute? Can you come to my office?"

Oh boy, here it goes. I am going to get fired.

"Augusta, you are an excellent worker, and you are always willing to go above and beyond. You are, however, the worst secretary I have ever had. You know you can't spell, right? I understand, and I empathize with you. I know this is happening because of your situation. I have to have someone out there who can do better."

Here it comes. I braced myself for the hammer to come down.

"Now you may be the worst secretary I have ever had, but you are very in good sales. You are a natural at it, and you are powerful with customer relationships, so you are fired as my secretary and hired as my new salesperson. Do you want the job? It only pays a little more even though I can't give you much money, but the training and education you will receive are priceless."

Yes, sir. Thank you, Nelson. When do I start?"

"Immediately—I have to get you away from that secretarial work as soon as possible. We will begin interviewing someone new right away, and you will share Jeff's office and start training."

Jeff, though friendly enough toward me, never really warmed up. I always felt he was a little threatened by me. He would always tease me, referring to me as a teacher's pet. I knew Jeff would hold back with the training, and I would be not much more than his little slave. That bull showed his horns more than once. That was when I took it as a challenge, and the game was on. I stole the position out from under Jeff. I was willing to work and be fair with anyone, but I did not and would not lie down knowing someone was looking to bury me because of their shortcomings. The worst thing someone could do to me was to underestimate me or try to hold me back.

Jeff, in time, felt the need to give his notice, and I took over the sales office and was on one occasion again approached by Nelson. "I have an opportunity for you, Augusta. I know you will want to jump on it the right way, but you need to speak to Luke first because it entails traveling quite a bit and being away from home. Do you think you would like that, and would Luke be all right with it? I mean, would he be okay with you traveling two weeks out of every month?"

Let me go? Let me? Wow, I have to have permission from my husband? My first reaction was anger replaced with concern, but I quickly said, "He will have no problem with it, and yes, I want to do this very much."

"Okay, give yourself a day or two and talk it over with your husband. The job is yours if you decide you want it."

I left work that day on cloud nine. I was so excited to have the opportunity to travel and see the world. Wow, who would have figured this would ever happen to me? I had to be one of the luckiest people; now, how to bring up the subject with my husband was another matter.

When I arrived at our house in the Estates, Luke was already out back, taking care of the promise he had made me if I married him. My horse—I forgot that I would not see and be able to ride my horse as much if I was traveling. As for Tabitha, how would she take the news? Luke was so over-the-top protective of me that he was never going to go for this.

Slowly I started to descend from my cloud in the sky. *How is any of this ever going to come to be?* The connection I had with my horse was priceless. Riding helped make me physically more energetic, and when riding, the rest of the world came second. The muscle spasms rarely showed their ugly head anymore. I still had pain, but it was part of my life. Someone else might allow this to limit them, but I never did. When I had a terrible day with the pain, Luke was always there to help me through it, and he never once made me feel like I was a burden. He was so good to me, and I knew it was because of him that I had gotten as far as I had. My breathing problems were under control as long as my inhaler was close by, but they were not gone completely and never would be.

My first reaction would be to run into the house, shouting, "I got a promotion at work today, and I get to travel and see the world!" I was a lot more humbled now, knowing this was only the best thing in the world for me at the moment but not for the ones I loved so much.

Luke could read me like an open book. "So what's up, Smiley?"

Everyone else called me Smiley, but not usually Luke. He lovingly called me Sparky. I sat down with Luke and Tabitha and announced my opportunity to both of them. Tabitha was the first to say she thought it was great. She also wanted to tell me that Grandma and Papa and Dad too wanted her to come there for the entire summer and holiday breaks now that she was older.

Luke was quiet, not saying much at all. "Augusta, I can see you want this, and no matter how much I do not want you to go and how much I am frightened for you, I know you want this, and every time I looked at you, I would feel guilty for being the one who took it away. Anyway, isn't this one of your visions? You will travel and see the world. I have learned through the years that even if I wanted to, I could not stop your predictions no matter what you have tried to do to alter what you have seen. It doesn't matter; you have only been able to change the path and make the choice of how to arrive, but you still always get there. Except for the job, we will be just fine."

I had five years of travel to and from the United States, Europe, and occasionally, South America. Returning to Florida with my family and my horses were great, and my life was good. The pay was still comical, and I found out how much of a joke as I got to know about the salaries of other salespeople in my field. However, Nelson wasn't lying. He said that the pay was terrible, but the experience would be priceless.

I knew this vision had come full circle. I felt it, and I was feeling that pull I could not control. I was fighting it as hard as I could to make it go away. I liked my life now, and it was a bit sad that I had to move on. I did not even know where exactly I was supposed to go, just that constant tug that was relentless. Everything was turning sour because I was fighting the change. I found out the owners of the hotels where I was working were ruled by greed and power, which I felt I was enabling by working for them. My daughter decided she wanted to move back to Connecticut and be on her own, and Luke was pressuring me to give up the horses because he could not find the time to take care of them all by himself when I was on the road. Luke's kids, now older, were smarter and more creative in their torments of me, and Luke became a workaholic, believing that if he became more financially independent, I wouldn't have to work and that I would be happy to just stay at home. Life would be like the *Little House on the Prairie*.

Everything started to unravel, even my health. I was depressed. With that came the pain in my body and the attacks of asthma that had hospitalized me several times. I knew that the time and reason for being in Florida to heal and travel to see the world was over. I knew it was time to leave the hotel and job position. If I chose to stay, I would be turning my back on the reality I was looking for. The final choice was mine to make. I would have to pay the price if I chose not to step out of my comfort zone. If I stayed, the marriage would be over in time, and I knew that because of the depression, the stepdaughters, the workaholic husband, and my adverse health, life was beginning to suck.

For two more years, I tried fighting the call for change. I did leave the hotel finally. I wanted to put it in its proper place—listening to my family, trying to conform, but still being in control of my own life. I tried to convince myself that all that nonsense about taking on another journey was perhaps all in my head. The past predictions that came to fruition were just odd coincidences.

I just worked at odd jobs in the area, not wanting to be sucked back into the hotel world, and the inner peace that had once been my steady best friend was gone. I could no longer see things. Life had become complicated and sad; not even my horse made me happy any longer.

Chapter 10

The Rolling Hills (2000)

Tabitha had moved back to Connecticut to stay with her father. He was a good father, just a bad husband who had another family now. He was more than willing to take her in against the wishes of his new wife. That lasted all of three months before Tabitha realized it was a wrong move and living with her father was impossible. She loved him—he was her father—but she did not like him very much at the time.

I was home that hot Florida winter morning when my daughter called. "Hello, Mom, I just wanted to call you and tell you how much I love you and understand now in a whole different way why we had to leave Daddy. There is something not right with him, and he seems so unhappy and mad all the time, and I'm pretty sure he is drinking too much. All they do is argue and fight. My stepmother blames it all on me, but I think they just look for excuses to fight, and I am a convenient target. They are never kind to me here."

I replied, "Tabitha, you are welcome to come home. Honey, Luke and I miss you."

"No, I need to stay here but not with him. Florida doesn't make me happy either, and as you have always taught me, Mom, if you are not satisfied, you are out of balance. If you don't like something, and it is in your power to change it, do it. If you do not, it is your fault."

Again, out of the mouths of babes.

I knew I had to stop trying to fight the pull that was telling me it was time to move on. I did not understand the urgency, only that I was being called. I tried almost every day to talk to Luke about it, but it was like he was utterly oblivious to my pain. I did not want to make his life complicated, and though I loved him with all my heart, I still had things to do. He closed his eyes to the stress I was under, not being accepted by his two girls and what they were putting me through. They would have done anything back than to manipulate their father and turn him against me. I would point out the things they were doing and the untruths they were telling, but no parent wants to hear anything negative about their children. I had reached the point that I was afraid to drink anything that had been opened in the refrigerator. I know that could have been paranoia on my part, but someone did place drugs in my soda one day when his daughters were visiting along with a few friends. The drug at the time was called Special K. I was frozen, unable to move as the evening unfolded. I was fortunate that day that there were other people present who took care of me.

"Luke, are you listening to me? Do you hear me? We need to leave this place!" I would say.

He would just say, "Calm down, Augusta. Everything will be all right."

I knew it was not going to be okay—the walls were closing in, and I started to have panic attacks. I was in a downward spiral.

Tabitha had moved out of her father's house now that she was seventeen, close to eighteen, and was welcomed into the home of her best childhood friend, Renee. Her family was good people and always loved Tabitha. I felt good that she had a safe place to go. Then the phone rang.

Tabitha called crying, not able to get the words out. "Mom, I'm pregnant."

"You're what! Oh my god, Tabitha, how could you let this happen?" Instantly I knew what a stupid question that was even as it left my mouth, but it was already out there.

"Don't be mad at me, Mommy. I am so sorry."

"Okay, honey, what do you want to do? Come home. We will figure this out together."

"No, Mom, I have decided to have the baby but not marry the father."

"Who is the father, Tabitha?"

"It is Robby, Renee's brother. It's a long story, but even though I am not going to marry him right now, the family says I can stay here and have the baby, and after the baby is born, we can get married then if we want to."

"Do you love him, Tabitha?"

I don't know, Mom. That is why I don't want to marry him right now, but I will have this baby, and I need to stay here. This is my responsibility, and I will make it right. This decision is my choice and my road to go down. I just don't want you to hate me or be mad at me. Dad has disowned me, and I feel so stupid and alone and scared."

"Tabitha, you're my daughter. I love you and would never hate you. You will always have a home here, and I am here if you need me, and I would like you to come home if you ever decide you want to. Please call me soon, and I need to hear from you often, okay?"

2001

Nine months went by quickly as I continued to ask Luke to leave Florida and go anywhere but there. I resented the fact that he was still in denial and had closed his eyes to all the negative energy that surrounded us. How could he not see this? He would also humor me from time to time with the possibility of leaving, but I figured out he was only giving me false hope to keep me quiet for a while. We were not going anywhere.

I stayed in constant touch with Tabitha, being a part of this critical time in her life by phone and pictures sent by email of her fast-growing stomach. The time was close for my grandson to be born. Tabitha wanted me there with her, and my bags were packed. Luke decided a visit back to the hometown would be excellent for me, and he would visit his family while there also.

Because there was only one real substantial income coming into the house these days, flying was not an option, so we decided to drive and knew that maybe we could not make the birth in time, but at least we would be able to see our new grandson when he was a day old. My presence was so crucial to Tabitha and me. I wasn't going to let her down.

We made it in time. The doctors had sent Tabitha home and said she had a day or two to go, so she was told to go back and relax, and they'd see her in a few days. She was already two weeks late.

A few days turned into five more. I spent as much time as I could with her, but Tabitha could not spend much time on her feet, which were the size of watermelons.

Road Trip

"Let's go on a road trip, Luke, and get away from this area for the day. The doctors said Tabitha is not supposed to go into full labor yet, so I want to take a pleasant drive out of this area."

So we did. We drove east, looking at the scenery as it became more rural with every exit we passed. Every time Luke would suggest we get off one of the exit ramps and get something to eat, I would say, "No, let's go a little farther."

"You know we are going to be in Massachusetts soon if we don't stop."

"Just a bit farther, okay? This feels right."

"What feels, right? Oh no, you are not starting this shit again, are you?"

"Yes, I am opening up this shit again." We began to argue. "You will not listen to me. After all this time, you know I have been right, yet you stay in denial, and you think you can just close your eyes to what we both know to be the truth. Close your eyes, and it will all go away if you ignore it. Well, guess what? It will not go away. You can ignore all the signs, but I am not going to." My heart was beating so fast, and I had this energy in me that I have not felt in a very long time. "Can we please go a little farther, and I will tell you what exit to get off?"

Exit 105! Luke got off of exit 105. "This is Stone, Connecticut, Augusta. There is nothing in Stone, Connecticut, Augusta. This is cow country. What do you expect to find here? Oh, I get it, you think the white house with the rolling hills and the water you saw in your vision is here, don't you? Augusta, we are inland. There is no water here like you described."

"Just keep going down this road, Luke. Humor me please. If we're supposed to find it, we will. If not, I'll shut up and go home."

"Well then, that's a deal. I will drive wherever you tell me to go if this will shut you up once and for all, and we can go home!"

"Hey, look where we are. We are on the university's campus. We are in Stone, Connecticut, Augusta. There is no water here unless that little pond over there is your water." He laughed at me.

"Shut up, Luke. That is not the water, but look over there. Are those not the rolling hills I described! They are perfect, and there, look—those are the three buildings exactly where I said they would be, and you can't close your eyes to that. That is the gold ball. So it was not a ball but a gold dome on the top of that building. When I was flying over the hills, it just looked like a big gold ball from my angle."

"Shit now, you are scaring me, Augusta. I have to admit that it all seems like it fits, but maybe we are just making it fit. I don't want it to be true. I want to have a regular quiet life as other people have. I do believe you, and I have always believed you because I have seen it with my own eyes. I have lived it with you. I know that not everything could be a coincidence. I just don't want to lose you, and I am not in your future visions. You don't mention me in the image to come. What happens to me? What happens to us, Augusta?"

Now I understood. Luke was afraid my time with him or maybe even on this earth was coming to an end, and he was trying to stop it or at least slow it down. I took his hand, reassuring him that just because the visions were not as bright as they progressed, it did not mean we were not together or that I was going to die. The future was fuzzy, maybe for a different reason, and we should not assume or try to figure out why. Every time people thought they knew what the plan was and how it was going to transpire, they got smacked in the face as if someone or something was saying, "Just go with the flow. It will happen when the time is right."

"We are close, Luke. The white house has to be just down the street a bit."

"All right, but I am telling you there is no water here."

As we drove down a big hill out of campus, I said, "It is here. I feel it calling me."

"Augusta, I sure hope you don't talk this way in front of anyone other than me because they would surely lock you up and throw away the key."

"Pull in here. This is it."

The car had not even come to a complete stop before I was jumping out with absolute excitement. Luke yelled, "You crazy idiot, what are you doing!" and stopped right in his tracks before the last syllable had left his lips. Behind the house was a long beautiful pasture, and behind that was a large body of water like a vast lake or most likely a reservoir. It had a line of evergreen trees across the backshore, just as I had described. I ran from the front to the back and up to the back porch, landing on the four cement steps to peer into the house windows.

"Augusta, stop it, what are you doing? This house belongs to someone. You just can't run around as if you own it. This house is not even for sale."

"The house is empty, Luke, and it is my house, or it is going to be our house."

Luke knew it was no use even trying to hold me back. *Damn if she wasn't right again,* he thought.

I saw that the house was empty as I cupped my hands together to make a spyglass against the windowpane. It had a little back entranceway with a small bathroom at the end, which held one of those stackable washers and dryers, toilet, and washbasin. On the left was a doorway—no door but led into another room. Only the corner of the room could be seen because the angle from where I was looking did not allow me to see much. There was a window to the left of me, but it was a little too high to see through. It must have been the window over the kitchen sink where one could prepare dinner while looking out over that beautiful body of water outback.

Luke decided to join in at this point and called me to the side of the house and up to two additional cement steps; this door led directly into the side entrance to the kitchen. There was a full-length etched-glass window for this door with no shade or curtain on it so you could see the entire kitchen. The house had lovely wooden floors that looked recently finished. All the appliances seemed relatively new also, or at least they were very well maintained. The kitchen had wooden cabinets and even a beautiful wine rack. This old house must have been recently remodeled. It was unique and something you might not see every day because usually all of the walls would be painted white or shell cream, making it easier for the prospective buyer to have a vision of their decorations in the house.

The kitchen had two distinct exits—open arches—and the one directly ahead most likely led to the dining room. This room was painted in a soft cream color and led to another room decorated with a muted evergreen color. The entire house had wooden floors. In the far left corner, one could see a closed door, \a door that could have led anywhere but Luke assumed it went to the basement.

I had made it back around to the front already. I was trying to see into the front door, but that was a little more difficult because it was a beautiful dark oak door that also had a white stained-glass window that made it very hard to see through, but one could make out a beautiful old wooden staircase that led upstairs.

The house was relatively small, maybe 1,000 to 1,200 square feet under the roof. It was white with black shutters, and it sat directly on top of the road. In place of a front yard, there was a beautifully crafted stone wall that separated the street and the house. The house had been there for years before the road came, and instead of knocking it down, they left it and made a wall to protect it from the fast-moving traffic. New England had so many old beautiful homes, and we wondered how old this one was.

Behind the house on the left was a massive white barn. It was twice the size of the house and built into the hill. A once-used outhouse with one toilet was disconnected from the barn and required significant repairs. The main entrance to the barn was on the street level, and the remainder was situated on the slope. The home, surrounded by landscaping, required care; it was overgrown but had possibilities and was shaded by a huge black walnut tree just to the right of the barn.

"Okay, Augusta, the house is here. The water is here. Your rolling hills are here, but there is no FOR SALE sign, so someone must have already brought it and just haven't moved in yet, don't you think? We do not have time to find out. We have to get back to your daughter. It is 4:00 PM and at least an hour-and-a-half drive back. It is Sunday, and real estate offices are probably not even open now. We leave Tuesday, so let's just go." As Luke took two steps backward to turn toward the car, he heard a crunch under his foot and looked down. Buried in the dirt and covered by the overgrown grass was a metal sign that was face down.

I smiled and said, "Oh yeah, have a little faith, Luke. There is your sign, and look, you helped discover it. It hid from all other prospective buyers, waiting for us to find it."

I dialed the number from my cell phone and said hello. The agent on the other end of the phone call was not willing to come out to show some out-of-town people a house on Sunday and pretty much blew us off. I wrote down the telephone number and the name of the agency and got into the car with Luke, feeling unfortunate and disappointed but not defeated. I felt like I was leaving a loved one behind as we pulled out of the driveway, and my eyes filled up with tears.

As we headed back the way we came, not more than a mile up the road on the right was a RE/MAX real estate office, and there was a car in the parking lot.

"Okay, Augusta," Like said, "let's stop in here and talk to someone, but I can't see how any of this matters. The whole exercise is fruitless. We can't buy the house. We still have jobs and a home in Florida, and we have no way to pull this off, so you are just getting yourself all excited and wasting this agent's time getting information about it. Then again, I should know better—you never cease to amaze me, and this has to be the most bizarre set of events I have experienced with you yet. Every time I have convinced myself that your visions have just been uncanny coincidences or you made them happen, something like this hits me in the face. I can't fight it. I am just along for the ride, I guess."

We entered the real estate office to speak with an agent.

"Hi, I'm Augusta," I said, "and this is my husband, Luke, and we were interested in getting information about the little white house for sale right down the street. It is not your listing, but that real estate person did not want to be bothered today, so we were hoping you could help us."

"Sure, my name is Eric, and I will pull the listing up on the computer and see what I can tell you about it." Luke and I sat in the chairs directly in front of Eric's desk, and he searched for the listing, printing out the specifications of the house.

"Well, the house was built in 1786 and was recently remodeled. It looks like the current owner gutted the inside and redid the whole thing. I am new here in this office but have not seen anyone at the house for the six months I have been here. The price is amazingly low. They are only asking $150,000 for it, and according to the report, only a few people have even asked about it in the past six months, so I bet the price is negotiable. Do you want to see it? The house doesn't have a lockbox on it, and the footnote says there is a key somewhere. I will call the listing broker and find out where. How interested are you? I do not mind showing you the house, but it is 4:30 PM on Sunday, and the only reason I happen to be here is that for some strange reason I left my cell phone here at 2:00 PM when I left the first time, and I had to come back to get it. I guess it was just fate that I returned just as you were headed back, huh?"

"Yes, it must have been fate. This might be your lucky day and not so fortunate for the agent who blew us off. Okay, let's go. I always wanted to see the inside of that house anyway."

Luke just kept quiet, letting me and Eric bond. He muttered under his breath again, only loud enough for me to hear. "I am just along for the ride anyway. Isn't that right, Augusta?"

As we pulled back into the driveway, I felt at peace, and a warm, welcoming feeling came over me as if the house was happy to see us again. A fresh warm breeze greeted us as the car door opened. The sweet smell of honeysuckles filled the air.

We went from room to room downstairs, and it didn't take too long to find that there were just four rooms—the kitchen, the half bath, the dining room, and the living room—as we moved up the stairs to the second floor. I paused abruptly. There was something I saw in my head.

"There is a loose board on the top of the landing with a sharp nail sticking out, so be careful not to step on it. The bathroom is an awful pink. What was the owner thinking? The back bedroom has a door that leads up to the attic. Something is off with that second bedroom," I stated. "I wonder why?"

Luke caught the puzzled look on Eric's face after my little speech, but Eric, protecting his possible real estate deal, rapidly dismissed the look and said, "So, Augusta, what was that you said?"

"Oh, nothing, just a silly thought, but there is a nail on the top landing, and someone will surely hurt themselves on it. We should get something to bang it back on the floor or pull it out."

As we turned the corner, in front of us were pink tiles from the floor halfway up the walls of the bathroom.

"Okay, I am just a little freaked out at the moment. How did you know that, Augusta?" Eric muttered in a low whisper as if he was afraid there might be others listening.

"Try living with her," Luke said spontaneously. "It is not easy being me," he said snickering.

"Oh, stop it, guys. I am just having fun with both of you. All old houses have loose boards with nails. I just got lucky, and I could see part of the bathroom tile through the outside window the first time we were here. I got you both, didn't I?" I rolled my eyes at Luke, hidden from Eric, and he just nodded his head ever so slightly as if to say "Good save."

Eric laughed aloud. "Oh, wow, yeah, you sure did. I was just about to tell you to be my guest and look around the house, and I would wait for you outside."

The bedroom to the right of the bathroom was about ten feet by ten feet; there was no closet, and it was painted a plain sterile white. It was the only one room. The bedroom directly across from the stair landing was very dark emerald green and no bigger than a more modern home's walk-in closet, maybe seven feet by eight feet. Luke pointed out that these rooms had no storage either, and Eric added that none of the older homes have closets. They did not have many clothes back then and just used credenzas and dressers. Two floor-to-ceiling windows had little white square panes and overlooked the side yard where you could see blackberry bushes. The bushes were hidden from someone's view when standing in the yard because they draped down behind the hill into the pasture below and the overgrown landscape covered them. The other window had a view of the water and field and was very picturesque.

"What about this third room?" Luke said. "Look closet, doors!" He opened it and found a very narrow staircase leading up into the attic. "Well, maybe someone could make the entire attic one big walk-in closet. As long as you don't gain any weight, you can make it up here, and it is enormous and has possibilities if someone wanted to take the time to finish it. Let's go down into the cellar and take a look at the pipes and the furnace. Maybe the owner put in a new one, and then I want to look at that great barn and walk around the property again."

"Well, we better do that pretty fast," Eric said. "I doubt if that old barn has electricity, and the sun is starting to go down quickly."

"Okay, come on, Augusta. Let's check out the basement."

I started for the basement door and stopped; I became very dizzy and nauseous. All the color rushed from my face, and I just about fainted. Luke caught me, and his physical contact with me snapped me back to alertness. I shook my head and said, "I think I want to skip the basement, you guys. Cellars were never my thing. I will be on the back steps. Hurry up so we can see the barn."

"Are you okay, Augusta? You don't look so good."

"Oh yeah, I'm fine. I think I just need to eat soon. You know we haven't eaten anything since morning." I was not going to tell Luke of the awful feeling of sadness and blackness I felt coming from that hole in the ground. I had no idea what was down there, but it was sucking the energy from me. I had to get some distance.

The barn was fantastic, with the main level twice the size of the entire house, and on either side, it had high lofts that could be gotten to by way of a built-in wooden ladder that looked surprisingly strong—it had to be at least a hundred years old. There were several trapdoors in the floor that opened to the place that one would throw down bales of hay to the livestock below without having to go down to the next level if he/she chose not to.

There were two ways down to the stalls below: the back stairs and, of course, one could walk down the patio stairs outside the back of the barn and reach the three large stalls that way. This barn was used mainly for cattle at one time. I was thinking horses, my horse, but the area that would have to be the paddock area was not level and had a gradual slant downward—not a significant problem for cows, but a horse could fall and break its leg.

It was getting dark now, and Luke asked Eric to get the rest of the information we were requesting about the house, and we would call him Monday morning. We got back into the car and phoned to see how Tabitha was doing and to tell Luke's mom that we would arrive at her house in a few hours and not to worry.

The phone rang not more than an hour after we got back to the house. Tabitha was undoubtedly on her way to the hospital this time, and my grandson was going to be born. "What a productive trip," I said as we got back into the car on our way to the hospital. "I get to witness the birth of my grandson, and I found my house! Isn't it just amazing how things transpired? If Tabitha hadn't moved back to Connecticut and got pregnant, I would not be here. If the baby were not late coming, we would have never gotten in the car to take a drive, and I would not have found the house, and if that FOR SALE sign was visible to the rest of the public, someone else might have brought it. If Eric didn't have to go back to the office just when he did, we would not have well. You get it, right?"

Tabitha and my grandson were both doing great, and we spent most of the next day with them at the hospital. In between, I was on the phone with Eric, getting the final information I needed on the house. I knew it was up to me to follow through because Luke, though he had been accommodating up to this point, in reality did not want to move and saw no way to make a move anyway. He did as much as he thought he had to and then was pretending again it was all just going to go away.

"Eric, I have to speak to Luke about all this, but I want the house, and I will call my brother as soon as we get back to Florida. He lives in Connecticut also and can help me find someone who could help me with a mortgage, so don't give up on me just yet, okay?" I wasn't sure how it was all going to work out, but I knew it was going to be. It would work out because this was the next step in my vision. I could not stop it even if I wanted to, which I did not. How could anyone not move forward on an image that had been with them since childhood? I felt alive again, happy, and excited.

In my mind that night, I said to the house, "Bye for now, but I will see you soon."

Luke was silent most of the way back home. Every time I tried to bring up the subject of the house and making a move, he would shut down. I did expect this and knew I might have to make this happen without him. I knew that it would be a bad idea to stay in Florida. Our marriage would be over, so why not pursue a new home?

I took the phone and called my brother. "Joe, can you help me buy a house in Stone, Connecticut? Do you have any friends in finance who could work wonders for me? I may have to do this on my own because Luke is not on board and has no intention of helping me."

"Okay, Augusta, I will see what I can do. My friend will call you by tomorrow."

I was waiting around Sunday morning for Joe's friend to call and try to talk to Luke about the whole thing, and finally, he broke down and said, "There's nothing I can do or say that's going to discourage you, Augusta—not when you've set your sights on something. I know you will not stop until you get what you want. I have known you long enough to very sure of that, but know this: I don't want this, and I will not help you. Augusta, if you go, you go without me. Are you ready to do that? I don't know why I am worried anyway because there is no way you can get a mortgage by yourself."

"Luke, I think you're worried because you do know me, and you know that if I say it is supposed to be, it most likely will be. I don't know why exactly, but I know if I try to stop it or if I don't recognize the signs that are leading me, I am doomed to be unhappy—unhappy enough to make me sick. If you truly love me, which I know you do, let me go. I want you to come with me, but yes, I am ready to go without you if you refuse to go with me. I have no choice, not really."

It seemed like an eternity, but it was only 1:00 PM when the phone rang. "Augusta, Jerry here. I understand you want to purchase another home, this one in Connecticut. Well, I worked miracles when you and Luke wanted to buy the house in Florida, so I can make this work if you just get the mortgage on your own without Luke. Your credit is excellent, and I have a lender that will take you on. Therefore, congratulations and welcome to Connecticut. We will somewhat be neighbors."

As I hung up the receiver, Luke was already walking out the patio door to the barn. I should have known. If you can't fight them, I guess you just have to join them.

"Muggsy, come on. Let's tell Mommy's horse, Sonny, that Mommy is going to leave."

Muggsy was the sweetest Great Dane and was very loyal to Luke. He got off the cold ceramic tile floor and followed Luke out the door as if he was snubbing me. They both headed for Sonny's stall, my Palomino mustang, who was very important to me to tell him the bad news.

"Excellent, Luke!" I yelled out to him. "Turn the animals on me now."

We had one month to get our finances in order and decide what items I would be packing in the truck and what would be left behind for Luke. Luke would drive the big vehicle while I packed up the smaller things in the pickup. We decided that we would stop by and get my sister Beth in Tampa for the long ride to Connecticut. The plan was not clear yet on how I was going to make all this work. Luke was being supportive enough to help me move forward, but he made it very clear that he would only be able to help me out minimally when it came to paying the bills in Connecticut. He had a house to maintain in Florida, and there was no way he could do both. It didn't faze me, and it was all going to work out and be all right because I was supposed to be there. I had already seen myself in the house, and this move was part of the master plan. So what is the master plan? I didn't know why I was just going with the flow.

The plan was that Luke would come to visit me once every four to six months and that he would put the house in Florida up for sale, and if it went quickly, he would just move in with one of his children or friends.

He had no timeline or promise to move there anytime soon. He said Muggsy would stay with him, but Sonny had to go to my friend's house in central Florida because he could not take care of him while I was doing whatever I was going to do in Connecticut. The barn at the new house had to be made ready for a horse, and fencing had to be put up, the land cleared, and electricity installed, etc.

"Augusta, you are living in a dream world. Honey, I love you to death, but are you sure this is what is supposed to be?"

"Why do you still question me, Luke? I did not ask for the sight. It was a gift though you probably think it was a curse. Has not everything I have said so far come to be? I don't know why I just know. I know I can't fight it. Every time I try to make it different and think I have turned the tide in a different direction, something bizarre happens, and I am forced right back on track. I do not know where I will end up. I am currently unaware of what I am supposed to do with all this, but I will know in time. I don't expect you or anyone to put up with this craziness. I am surprised you did not leave me a long time ago or that someone else has not tried to have me committed. Still, the truth is you and most everyone else close to me know what has happened and is happening. The whole thing has much too much truth to be overlooked entirely. When I think that a person needs to believe in my predictions, he/she will because I will provide a reason for them to believe. I'm going to teach them and you that there is additional knowledge out there that no one can just walk away from without looking back. If it has no importance, it doesn't matter anyway."

"So why am I here, Augusta, just along for the ride? What is my role in this whole adventure of yours?"

"Luke, without you, I would not have been able to get this far. You are my rock, and you are my enabler. You knew the first time we met—well, the second time anyway—what I was. I told you everything. I held back nothing, yet you chose to stay. You must have believed me. Otherwise, you would have run away like an escaped rabbit that was about to be captured in a twisted cage. We all have free will, and I will never hate you for wanting a more rational, predictable life without me. I just can't have that. It is not possible. If you stay with me, I can only promise you my love. This time apart will be good for both of us. I have to concentrate on what has pulled me here and why this house. I am supposed to be working among children, which makes me laugh because I don't even particularly like kids. I can't imagine what kind of job is going to make me money and put me among the children, but I guess I will find out soon enough. I will find a job bartending or being a food server or something like that while I see what this all means. I am not worried about it though part of me screams you sure the hell should be concerned. Luke, if you are supposed to be here eventually with me, you will be. I have all the time in the world or at least until the rest of my predictions come full circle. I don't know what happens after that. I don't think I have given that part much thought because it seems to be a long way off, but my ending visions, as I have told you, are not real pretty, and I don't understand why I was I given this knowledge when there seems to be nothing I can do about it."

Chapter 11

Moving In

I asked my sister Beth to drive to Connecticut with us and help move me in. We would fly her back to Florida whenever she wanted to return. She was excited about making the trip to Connecticut and spending time with me. We talked and laughed and made Luke pull over in the truck behind us several times more than he would have liked so that we could visit the rest stops.

As Beth dozed off somewhere in South Carolina, I had time to reflect. It finally struck me that for the first time in ten years, I was going to be away from Luke. I would be on my own, apart from my dog and my horse. My heart started to pound, and panic set in. Oh my god, what have I done! What am I doing? What do I know about the area? What kind of people lives around here? Are there stores? Will there be any jobs? Will I be able to make friends?

I just dove in headfirst, not even worrying about any of those things. I didn't even know why the owner had decided to sell the place. Why was such a cute grand old house still available anyway? Have I made a horrible mistake? I questioned if I being reckless and a lot of crazy. As I started to hyperventilate, my cell phone rang; it was Luke calling Beth and me. He was driving directly behind us.

"How are you doing there, Sparky?" He hadn't referred to me as Sparky recently.

It brought a smile to my lips, and I answered him with, "I love you."

It was Sunday night around 10:00 PM by the time we reached the exit to my new home. Everyone was exhausted, and we made plans to spend the night at the Best Western right down the street from the house. The closing was to be at ten the next morning.

We slept like logs in the little inn and woke up raring to go when the sun came up. We knew we could start unloading the truck before the closing because a key to the house would be concealed in the shed under a flower pot. We passed a grocery store, a small mall with a gas station, and a bank. There was a whole life around me. Thank goodness for the little things. I hadn't made a complete mistake. As the moving van and the pickup pulled into the driveway, an incredible calmness came over me. I was home. I was happy, and I was part of the house.

Luke was very organized and had a plan. He always had an idea; his life was one big thought-out plan that was continually interrupted by my spontaneity. He would stop me from jumping off cliffs, and I would prevent him from growing roots wherever he planted himself.

The plan was to back the truck right to the front door. The boxes came off the truck first and were placed in the kitchen where we could sort them out later. The little bit of furniture we had divided up was next. The house had no blinds or curtains on the windows, and this was not good seeing that we were sitting on a well-traveled road. Neither of us had thought about that until we entered the house this second time.

Time just flew by, and it was going to take about forty-five minutes to get to the closing location, so Beth said she would stay behind and empty some of the kitchen boxes while we were gone. We assumed we would be back no later than 1:00 PM.

I felt sad when we pulled out of the driveway, looking back at the house. I said to myself softly, "Don't worry. We will be right back."

"Who are you talking to, Augusta?"

"Oh, no one, just the house, it doesn't want me to leave."

"Oh, all right, you are a real nut case, you know."

"Yeah, I know, but you love me, right?"

We were the first ones there; the current owner of the house had not arrived yet. I signed all the paperwork I had to sign, and then the owner walked in. I was startled. The skeleton was so evident on his face. He was so young—maybe in his thirties.

"Oh my god, he is dying, and soon," I whispered into Luke's ear. "I see it."

"What are you talking about, Augusta? He is just thin, but he doesn't look ill to me."

"He is sick, honey, and he doesn't have long. That answers my question about why he is selling the house."

Luke spoke up immediately and said, "Hello, can I ask you why you are selling the home? It looks like you just recently put a lot of money into it with a new furnace, water heater, new wood floors, new washer, and dryer. Have you been there long?"

"Hi, David is my name, and the house is just not right for me. I only lived in the house for a short time while I renovated it. It was just too noisy."

"Yes," said Luke, "being so close to the street, I can see that traffic noise being a nuisance."

"Yes, that is it, the noise from the street," David said.

All the paperwork was completed, and we were getting ready to leave. I inched my way over, placing my hand on David's shoulder and said quietly, "How long did the doctors say you have, David?"

"Is it that evident that I am terminally ill?"

"No, not to most, but I know. It will be okay—I promise you. I am sorry for your illness, but know there is life beyond this one, and if you would like to talk, please visit me. I would love for you to come by and tell me all about the house."

David's eyes swelled up and turned away before the tears started to fall from his eyes, and he said as he turned, "I can tell you are a good match for the house. Be happy there, and if I can, I will take you up on that visit."

Luke pulled me away and said, "Could you not just leave it alone?"

"No, Luke, I could not. He was hurting, and he is frightened and needed to know I understood and that he was not alone if he did not want to be."

"Oh, your poor sister. This took a lot longer than we thought it would, and it is nearly 3:00 PM, and it is going to take us at least another forty-five minutes to get home. I have tried to phone her several times, but she doesn't answer her cell phone. I hope she is all right."

"I'm sure she is. Maybe her battery is just dead, or she forgot to turn the phone on. Yeah, that's it."

We pulled up to the house close to 4:00 PM to see Beth sitting on the stone wall in front of the house, looking very disturbed.

"Hey, we are so sorry it took so long. We tried to call you, but you did not answer your phone."

"Well, that would be because the phone is inside, and I am out here locked out! I have been out here for hours, just the cat and me."

"What cat?" I said.

"He is around here somewhere. He took off when you pulled in."

"Oh no, you got locked out. What happened?"

"Well, I ran out of the house as the doors slammed and locked behind me. I tried all the entries. I am not so sure I even want to go back inside that house."

"What the hell are you saying? Did something happen to you?"

"Yes, a lot has happened, Augusta. I've got a bad feeling that something isn't right with this house, and the house wanted me out, so I'm out."

"I am sure there is a very reasonable explanation. Let's see if we can find a way in to get your phone and grab my other purse so we can all go and get something to eat down the street." I reached for the handle; it turned, and the door opened.

"I am telling you that the door was locked, Augusta. I tried everything to get back in. All the doors were locked!"

"You know this is an ancient house, and the doors probably stick. I am sure they would not open. I am not questioning you at all. They are open now, so let's get what we need and go eat. You can tell me why you think there is something wrong with the house over dinner."

As we entered the front door hallway, we looked at each other in confusion when we saw at least four to five boxes opened and the contents all over the floor. We had set up the living room with furniture, and it was now sitting in the dining room; the TV was away from the wall and unplugged. Beth took her wallet and phone and said, "I'm going to wait for you in the car" and hurried out the front door.

"Luke, don't look at me that way. Say what is on your mind."

"Augusta, you know better than me that there is most probably a twist to this whole house thing, and there is something not quite right. You dreamed about this house, or you saw it in a vision. You found the house. You were able to buy it against all the odds. You knew every room and every nail sticking out of the floorboards. Yes, you might have gotten away with convincing Eric that it was all very logical and scientific, but I know better. This house seems happier and feels different when you are here. Even I can feel it. I can't wait to hear what Beth has to say. Look at the poor thing. She is frightened to death, waiting in the car. How are we going to get her to spend the night here with us? How are you going to convince her it is all right? I am the last person to believe in all this crap because I don't want to consider it. If I allow myself to give in to this mumbo jumbo paranormal stuff, I would have to accept all the awful predictions you have told me, and honestly, I would rather not know."

"We have to come up with a plan. I don't feel right leaving you here alone. I am frightened for you, and I don't understand why the hell you are so calm. It is like you are under some kind of a spell, just being led around like a zombie. The next time I come up, I am bringing the dog. At least he will be an excellent protective company for you."

"Okay, calm down. We are all hungry. It's been a long day, and we still have so much to do. You are only here with me for two days, and I need you to help me. After dinner, can we stop at the store and get a bolt for that cellar door. I need a lock on the outside, a solid one, okay?"

"What about the attic? You want one for that too?"

"No, the attic doesn't bother me. I like it up there."

There were only two choices for eating: a McDonald's and a little pizza joint up the street. The vote was for pizza. We had enough fast food to last a lifetime on the ride up from Florida. No one said much until the first full slices hit all of our stomachs.

"Okay, Beth, it is time to tell us what happened," I blurted out.

She said, "I was standing in the kitchen and saw a yellow tabby cat out on your backyard stone wall. He was meowing at me."

"Yes," I said, "that is the cat that Luke and I saw the first time we saw the house. He came right up to us, and it seemed like he belonged here. As a joke, we put on the real estate offer papers that we wanted the light fixture in the dining room to stay as well as the cat. We thought that was funny, but the owner said that the cat had always been here even when he moved in, so he just fed him. The cat would never come into the house no matter how much he tried to lure him in. He said the cat belongs to the house, so yes, if you want him, the cat stays."

"Augusta, you know my love for cats," said Beth, "and I had guessed someone has been feeding him because, for some unknown reason, I knew that there was a bag of cat food in the pantry, so I brought out some food and a bowl of water to him. He sat there and ate the food. I called him Missa. I don't even know what that is. I thought I saw something in the kitchen window, just for a second mind you, but when I looked that way and then back to the cat, he was gone. I went back inside and started to empty some boxes. I was standing at the kitchen sink and felt something close by, something playing with my hair. I swear to God, Augusta, my hair was moving, and I had goosebumps up and down my arms and felt a cold breeze enter the room. I laughed at myself, took a deep breath, and continued putting the glasses in the cupboard. The TV was off."

Beth then asked me if I knew that the cable company had already connected our service. She said that she did not even know that the cable company had already been here or if they had turned on the service but knew that she did not turn that TV set on. The music station was playing, and it was loud. "I could not find the remote to turn it down, so that is why you saw all those boxes in disarray. I was looking for the remote for the TV. When I finally got the volume down and things were quiet, I heard something upstairs like banging. I thought to myself, *Don't go up there, Beth. You know you are not supposed to go exploring old creepy houses when alone.* But I did not want to be a big baby. Plus, I was going to be alone for a while, and I had to check it out. The back door was open, so I assumed maybe the cat came in and was upstairs, so I went up. By the way, there is a loose board up there with a nail sticking out. Someone could get hurt. I went up, and it was cold. It was frigid. It's June, no air conditioning, no windows open, so why so bitter cold? I saw nothing, but I swear to God I heard someone giggle, and then the TV went back on loud—really, really loud. I ran downstairs, and the chairs that you put in the living room were now in the dining room facing the wall. I unplugged the TV and raced to the front door, which, by the way, was now open to me! When I got outside, the door slammed behind me, and I heard the back door slam also. Where you found me on the stone wall is where I have been ever since. I did try to get back in to get my phone, but none of the doors would open. I even tried to knock on the doors of the couple of neighbors you have, but no one seemed to be home. My next move was walking down to the inn we stayed at last night, but I kept telling myself you guys would be back real soon, and I should wait. I'm telling you, you bought a haunted house. You're crazy if you live there."

"Let's be rational for a minute. I bet some neighbor kids have been having some fun with you. They have probably been using the empty place as their playhouse and found it amusing to scare you. There has to be a logical explanation, and that is the best one I can come up with right now. It is too late not to move in, and I feel good and at peace in the house even if there are ghosts. I don't believe they mean us any harm. They just have to learn to share the house with me," I said and kind of laughed.

Luke paid the dinner bill, which was very high compared with Florida prices, and mumbled, "Welcome to Connecticut. I swore I would never come back to this state, and here I am. Well, at least for the next two days. Don't worry, Beth. I will protect you from the house and the ghost. I will kick their asses if they pull any shit with me. Let's go back. You can sleep with Augusta tonight, and I will sleep on the blow-up bed. We will put some loud rock music on while we put the bed together and put the furniture back in the living room and let Augusta sing. That might scare them enough to leave."

"Ha, ha, hilarious, Luke. Be careful, or I will tell them to get you."

The night went off without a hitch, no weird noises, no cold spots, no cat anywhere around, and I slept better than I had slept in months.

I was up at the crack of dawn, found the coffee pot, and the box of donuts and bagels they picked up the day before at Dunkin' Donuts. Beth and Luke were up shortly after, ready to start their day. It was such a beautiful day. The kitchen window overlooked the pasture below, which was green and breathtaking; I could just imagine running through the grass, letting the sun hit my face. The reservoir right beyond the field was deep blue with only the slightest current and looked very inviting, but I was told that I could look but not touch because that was the town's water supply and this section of the reservoir was off-limits to all. How disappointing because of how wonderful it would be to have a little boat and dock in the backyard to float on and enjoy the fresh breezes. I was happy though to at least have this beautiful view. Even Luke and Beth were mesmerized by the spectacular vistas. *They both seemed a lot more peaceful and settled now. They just needed a good night's sleep and relaxation after being on the road for so many days,* I thought to myself. Beth even agreed that maybe, just maybe, she imagined some of what happened the day before or at least that there was only an unknown logical explanation for the disturbances.

Luke's real love was outside work. He was not much for the inside stuff, so after he secured that extra-heavy-duty lock on the cellar door, he found an excuse to go outside. He called into us, "Did you see the garden that was once here, on the hill? It needs a lot of work, but I bet it could be beautiful again. Look, there is an old well. I wonder if it is working. There are ancient blackberry bushes. These kinds of blackberries are hard to find. They are like the original stock. Look at this walnut tree in the backyard. This tree has to be a least 150 years old. Look how big the base is."

Beth and I ran from window to window, looking out as Luke kept yelling to us about all the new things he was finding. I smiled and knew it might take a while, but he would join me eventually. The house had gotten his interest and found his soft spot. I thought to myself, *The house is smart, a real smart home.*

I was just about to turn away from the window when a beautiful breeze came through; the scent of honeysuckles filled the air. "Luke, are there honeysuckle bushes out there somewhere?"

"I don't see any, Augusta, but I found big black grapes, wow! They are ripe and sweet. This is not the time of the year for grapes, is it?"

He was out of our sight now, inside the barn, and Beth said, "I can see why you love this place, Augusta. Boy, you have a lot of guts doing this on your own. I envy you your new adventure. You are acting on your gut feelings, which most people never dare to do."

"Well, don't give me too much credit. You know my story. I did not choose this house. It was waiting for me."

"All right, let's not get back on that kick again. Let me just enjoy the time here with you."

"We finished putting away all the big stuff in the house already. The rest is just me pitter-pattering around, and because I don't have a job yet, I will have plenty of time for that. Let's find out what Luke is doing. He went into the barn a while ago. Let's make sure he is all right. He is a bit of a natural disaster these days."

We went out the back door and down the four little cement steps to the next set of wooden steps that led to the back of the barn. Luke was standing over some kind of vat—a twelve-foot-by-ten-foot cement hole in the ground that had a severe concrete lid; one would need a crane to uncover it.

"I wonder what the hell this is," he said.

"Maybe this is an old well," I said.

Luke said, "I don't think so. Even if it were an old dried-up well, it would be on the plot plans for the house. There is nothing on the plot plans that says anything about this thing. Well, maybe there are a bunch of dead bodies in there, or it is where they used to plow in all the cow shit until it became fertilizer. This place was a cow farm a long time ago, right?"

"Yeah, you may be correct. This top is just too damn heavy for someone to use more than once a year. I am sure we will find out eventually. So what do you think, Luke, will we be able to turn this old cow barn into a horse barn?"

Luke looked pleased with the possibilities: "Yeah, this is a grand old barn, nicely built, and there was running water in there at one time. I will show you where the sink was. There is a little stall on the left of the center one. They must have kept either goats or baby calves in there. Look, each section has trapdoors that lead upstairs. They would unload the grain or the hay and just drop it down—pretty cool."

Beth and I were checking out all the trapdoors in the ceiling above us when Luke vanished. "Where did you go?"

"I'm up here!" Luke screamed. "This must lead to the upper level of the barn. It's like three floors. Wow, come up! This place is massive. It'll fit a hell of a lot of hay and make a great apartment someday."

Beth hopped up the stairs first, skipping every other step, and as I headed to the stairs, I again smelled honeysuckles and felt a strange warm breath on the back of my neck; something was right on top of me holding me back, stopping me from moving forward. I didn't feel threatened; I felt protected. I wanted to call out for Luke, but nothing would come out. Just as Beth hit the last step reaching the main floor landing, the staircase started to break loose from the wall and rip apart. The whole thing just let loose and fell into pieces on the ground right in front of my feet.

"Oh my god, what just happened? Augusta, are you all right? Augusta, where are you?"

The force that held me from getting onto those stairs released me, and I yelled out to Luke, "I'm all right! I am right here! I was not on the stairs—someone, something stopped me," I added under my breath, not loud enough for either of them to hear.

"What the hell, those stairs were solid! What the hell happened? Why would they fall apart like that? Come around to the front," Luke said. "Augusta, do not go anywhere near those steps. I am going to have to have a builder come out here and make sure the rest of this place is safe. That damn house inspector should have picked up that those steps were dangerous. Now I am going to worry that you will be lying somewhere in this barn or that old house all alone and injured, and you don't know anyone, and no one knows you for them to realize you are even missing."

"That was just a freak accident, Luke. You worry too much. I am fine, not a scratch on me, see. I will make friends and get to know the neighbors. I will not be alone—I promise you. I feel very safe here for some strange reason. Thank you, whoever you are, who protected me. I hope we can be friends." I turned to go back the way I came.

Luke opened the side barn door, which was locked from the inside. "Strange," he said to himself and us. "The reason why we could not get in to see the barn the first time we were here was because there is a bolt-on the inside of the door."

"Maybe they came in from that big sliding door right here," Beth said, "though it doesn't look like it has been opened for a very long time. Look how rusted the tracks are, and the door is not even on the hinges. That should cost a pretty penny to get fixed."

"Well, the last person in here must have locked up and gone downstairs and out the back way, right?"

"Yeah sure, whatever you say, Augusta," Beth said as she rolled her eyes.

I threw my sister a look of disapproval and betrayal. "Let's look at that garden. Look, here is a spade and shovel just waiting for us. Hey, Luke, take a look at this ladder. It seems like someone made it. Wow, made all of the wood and tied together like they used to do it back in the 1700s."

Luke went around the front of the house. Beth and I went to the back where the old well was located—the one recorded on the plot plan, which was functional—and the hill that was once a beautiful garden. We kneeled to take a look at the soil and see what might still be alive. As we played in the garden, turning over the ground to see if the roots of the flowers were savable, the smell of honeysuckles again filled the air.

"Do you smell that?" Beth said.

"Oh yes, I smell that. It makes me feel safe and happy for some reason, but I don't see any honeysuckles around, so where are they?"

"I don't know. I am sure we just have not discovered them yet. Look how overgrown everything is. The bush may be hidden somewhere on the property or maybe next door, and the breeze is bringing the fragrance over here."

As we turned back around to tend to the garden, Beth gasped, "Oh my god! Look!"

I quickly turned to see what was so urgent in my sister's voice. The garden started to bloom right in front of our eyes. One big white flower where there was only a stem before was staring right at us, and a small honeysuckle bush was right there blooming.

"Now come on, Augusta, you have to admit that it is just plain weird and a little scary. I think the house is happy you are here, Augusta. Now you can't tell me there is not something going on here."

"Sure, I knew the minute I found the house, but you've got to understand that this home is another step in a bigger picture. Coming here has been a part of my life for a long time. I need to be here. I need to figure out the reason for all this and why. I think I've got to let go of what I've been told and stop playing safe. The house has plenty to teach me. Please don't say anything to Luke about the flowering garden because he's still angry at me, and now his fear is ramping up with the stairs caving in. He is just about ready to start hyperventilating. It is only his anger with me that is stopping him from staying here. He secretly hopes I will fail and come to my senses and run back to Florida. He knows he can't make me, so he is in his way trying to play a mind game with me. Can we just keep this between us? That is why I wanted you here and not one of our other sisters because you understand better than they do. Okay, do you promise?"

"Yes, I promise, but I think you are crazy to stay here, especially by yourself, but you seem to be so happy, and you say you feel safe, right? Anyway, who am I to try to stop the paranormal life you live. Just promise me you will be careful and know that good and evil are very close cousins. I think this place has both. I have a terrible feeling I can't shake, and at the same time, I don't know. I just don't know."

"Hey, there is someone in the house!" Luke yelled.

"What do you mean, Luke? Where?"

"I saw someone standing in the window right there. A girl, I think. Didn't you see her?"

"No, I didn't." Being the closest to the steps, I sprang up to look, not even stopping to think that maybe there was an intruder and I should be cautious.

"Augusta, wait a minute, you idiot. Wait for me."

I did not stop, and I felt an anger rage inside me that someone might be in our house, and all sense of reason was gone. The back door opened as I reached for the handle, and I sprinted through the hallway into the kitchen. "Hello, hello, is anyone here?"

Luke was right on my heels, but as he reached the door, it slammed shut, almost hitting him in the face. *What the hell?* The door was now locked, and Luke went into a panic, concerned about my safety. He banged so hard on the window that the glass shattered. He felt a sharp pain running down his arm. The pieces left behind on the doorframe were smudged by a bloody fist print. Beth ran to rescue him. She was so good at this kind of thing and had always been the family's caregiver. She just had that way, unlike me who seemed to be lacking in the nurturing department.

I was running from room to room, looking for the unseen intruder and heard whispering coming from behind the basement door. I felt faint and nauseous and drained. "Shit, I think they are down in the basement!" I yelled to Luke.

"Open the goddamn door, Augusta!" he yelled.

I pulled myself together, coming back to the land of the living, and ran to the back door and quickly opened it. "It's not locked. What happened?" I saw the blood running down his hand and arm, which my sister was trying desperately to look after.

"The door slammed in my face and then locked. I couldn't get in," Luke said.

"Well, it must have just gotten stuck because it is not locked. See, it isn't locked. I think I heard something in the basement, Luke. I thought we had the door locked with the bolt, right? Well, it is unlocked now, and I heard voices."

"Okay, you two stay outside and give me that shovel." Luke bravely entered the house, bloody hand and all, and started for the basement door, which was now ajar. He yelled out the open window. "Augusta, the door is open! Did you open it?"

"No," I said in a small panic. "Don't go down there, Luke, please. I have a terrible feeling."

"Fuck that shit. If someone is down there, they are going to pay for this. I'll beat the crap out of them."

There was a pause, and then Beth and I could hear Luke's footsteps as he slowly descended the wooden staircase until we could hear nothing more. "Are you all right? Do you see anything? Answer me, Luke. Are you all right?"

"Yeah, I'm fine. There is nothing down here, and there isn't any place to hide either. I am coming up. I think we are all letting our imaginations get the best of us. Look at us—you would think we moved into a haunted house just because it is old, and we are all still on edge because of that staircase collapsing in the barn. Let's clean up this cut of mine and get something to eat, all right?"

"Okay," we both meekly agreed.

Luke's cut was more like a gash; Beth thought he should get stitches, and I tried to make light of the matter by pointing out that though there was not much around there, there was a hospital about a half-mile down the street. It was not a standard hospital like you usually see, but it did say HOSPITAL on the white painted sign that hung by the entrance.

"How perfect and convenient is that, Luke? They must have known you were coming."

"Ha, ha, Augusta, but thanks, I don't need a doctor. I'll be just fine."

Beth laughed and said, "That's good because I believe that is a psychiatric hospital."

"Time for dinner," I said. "How about cooking up that chicken we brought with some baked potatoes and beans? How about a salad, Beth? You start on that. Isn't the vista so beautiful here? Look how pretty the pasture is this time of day and the sun setting over the lake."

"I don't think that is a lake," Luke said. "I believe it is a reservoir, and that is why you are not allowed on it."

"Well, that makes sense, but it still is beautiful to look at even if you can't touch it. It would be great to build a deck out there someday right off the kitchen. Then we could sit out there and just look. Don't you think so, Luke?" I was trying to reach his love of home and his male pitter-pattering desires and to form an image of what life might be like when he decided to join me eventually. He would eventually join me. I knew. I just did not know how long it would take him to realize we were both meant to be there. I was not supposed to be alone. He was part of my life, and I was very much his.

Night fell slowly, and the full moon cast a reflection onto the reservoir; the windows were open, and a cool breeze made the sheer curtains dance with such grace and peacefulness that one could not help but feel relaxed and happy. Well, that was the way I felt anyway. Beth still had the heebie-jeebies, and Luke was popping aspirin to ease the pain from his previous adventure.

Beth reminded us she had to catch an early flight back to Florida the next day, and we all had to be up before dawn. "I don't want to sleep alone, Augusta, and I hate to pull you away from Luke, especially when he has to leave in two days. Still, unless we can all find a way to sleep in the same room, I insist you sleep with me in the queen bed please, please, please. I can't be alone. I am sorry. I know you love it here and all, but really, something is just not right here! Come on, you guys—especially you, Luke—no one is saying it out loud, but I know you are all thinking it. This house is fucking haunted from the attic to the basement."

"All right, Beth." I closed my eyes deep in thought. "I admit something is going on, but I don't think it is mean. I was called here for a reason. I am supposed to be here, and so far, they have saved me from those stairs in the barn."

"What do you mean they saved you from the stairs?"

"Oh well, someone or something held me back, stopped me from getting on those stairs. I felt so protected, and I smelled those honeysuckles again at the same time, warm, peaceful, and safe."

"Well, that is just great, Augusta. The house is protecting you and attacking me. I guess you are supposed to be here, and I am not. Is that what you are telling me? Is that what you are feeling? What about Beth? What plans does the house have for her? Come on, guys, you are both freaking me out. I just want to get through the night and go home, and, Augusta, I know it is pointless to tell you to leave this place, but at least you know how I feel and what I think. I only hope you still have a relationship with God, and he protects you."

We all agreed to sleep in the same room. Taking one of the twin mattresses off the bed in the spare room, we made it up in the corner of the master bedroom, which was a lot smaller than the extra room; even I got an uncomfortable feeling in that room and chose not to make it the master bedroom. The so-called third bedroom was no bigger than a walk-in closet, and that was just what it was going to become, seeing that the house had not one closet anywhere like most houses built in the 1700s.

We settled in for the night, and I don't even remember my head hitting the pillow. Beth and Luke tossed and turned and freaked out over every little noise and creak they heard.

The Dream

It was cold, with snow on the ground. There was a whipping wind. I was in a wagon along with many others, all huddled against one another to keep warm. I think it was me as everything I saw was through those eyes. Still, it did not look like me. I was male, and I was wearing rags and was dirty, and the people all smelled as if they were rotting and diseased. The wagon was being pulled by two underfed horses that were weak and were being whipped by a horrid toothless man who made them pull this overweight wagon through the snow—to where was not known to me.

We passed many others who stood by the side of the path, crying and reaching out to their loved ones in the wagon only to be pushed down by soldiers guarding the cart. It felt like death. What did it mean? I could feel the cold, and the rags that covered me were rough against my skin, and they smelled of urine and dried blood. I could hear the voices speak a strange dialect; it was English but very different from the English I spoke. We were going to our death, I knew. "Help me please someone help me!"

"You're dreaming!" Luke's voice saved her from this god-awful dream that seemed so real.

"Oh, I had the worst nightmare ever. It seemed so real like I was there, Luke. They were taking me to my execution and grave. People were there trying to save their loved ones, but I was all alone. No one was there crying for me. It was awful," I said as I hung on to Luke's neck, never wanting to release him.

"Well, it was just a bad dream, Augusta. Do you want something to drink?"

"Yes, thank you. That would be great."

As I released my arms around his neck so that he could get out of bed, I screamed, horrified. It was not Luke. It was a man with white hair and a full-faced beard. His eyes were full of sad concern, and he reached out for me. I searched for my voice to scream and run only to be stopped by Luke once more. Or was it Luke? How could I be sure? Was I still sleeping? Was this real?

"Am I awake? Am I awake!" I screamed.

"Yeah, it's me, Augusta. You were crying and running around in your sleep. What was your dream?"

Beth huddled up in the corner of her mattress on the floor with a look of confusion. I had jumped right on her as I hurried away from the mysterious man who had held me in bed just a few minutes earlier. "I don't know. I just know it felt real and so sad, and then I thought it was you who was comforting me, and it wasn't you. It was someone else, and that felt real too and, and, and . . ." I could not find the words.

"Shush, calm down. Let's all go downstairs and get something to drink."

"That's what he said just before. Never mind. Let's just go downstairs."

"You're not leaving me up here alone." Beth said. "I am up for the rest of the night, and we have to get up in an hour anyway, so it might as well be now. I just want to go home."

I hugged my sister. "I am so sorry I stepped on you and that this trip was so awful for you and that you are afraid. I am all right, and I am going to be okay. Just a new house and the first time I know I am going to be alone for a while. I guess it all just came out in a weird dream."

"Well, I am just worried about you, Augusta," Beth said, "and for the record, it has not been awful. It was good most of the time. Just yesterday afternoon and last night sucked a big one."

We descended the wooden stairway onto the hallway's large-plank wooden floor that creaked with each step we took leading to the kitchen. Had we forgotten to shut the kitchen window, or did we? The breeze was constant and robust, blowing the curtain, and following it was that oh-so-faint sweet smell of honeysuckles. It was comforting and brought a smile to everyone as we looked and laughed at one another, shaking our heads.

The coffee was terrific—everyone agreed. We had two hours to get to the airport, so we had better leave at 5:00 AM, which was in fifteen minutes. I hugged my sister hard and long as if it might be the last time I would see her, or at least I knew it was going to be a long time before I saw her again.

When we got to the airport, she entered through the airport security gate and was gone. The drive back to the house was a quiet one. Luke was deep in thought, and I had gone from being panicked the night before to being excited and fearless about my upcoming adventure as if this was a long-overdue vacation that I had waited for my whole life. Luke was the one to break the silence. "Augusta, I do not want to be here, and I don't want you here either. You can't make it here on your own, and you don't even have a job. You are hours away from any family, and you have no friends here. What are you going to do in this creepy old house that hates me? How are you going to pay the bills? The mortgage is in your name, so it's your credit score that's going to be on the line. I don't even know how it happened. If you fail, and you will, I'm going to be home where you belong. Just don't take too long because I have a life to live."

"Are you threatening me, Luke? You have no plans or intention to join me here? So if I don't come back to Florida, you want a divorce? Is that what you want? Tell you what, you go back to Florida and spend time with your kids without me. We will see how long it takes you to understand that there were many reasons for me being here, not just the universe dragging me here. Some earthbound forces were pushing me also. You let me know when you figure that out. It is good that you are leaving. We both need time and space to figure out a lot of things. I can't have you around protecting me all the time, and maybe without me about, you will learn how to be a husband and less a father."

"What the hell is that supposed to mean?"

"You figure it out," I said as I slammed the truck door. I went to the back door entrance to the house, which slowly opened for me as I approached. Looking back, I was oblivious to it until it shut on its own and locked. I smiled and said under my breath, "Thank you, thank you very much."

"Augusta, unlock the door and let me in please. I don't want to fight with you. Let's just talk and have a good day together before I have to leave tomorrow. Please open the door."

I sat in the living room very pleased and smirking to myself. I said, "Guess we should let him in. Let's be kind to him, for he is leaving tomorrow, and we want him to go on a good note."

I smirked a little more to myself, thinking, *I bet I don't even have to get up to open the door, but let's not do that and freak him out even more. Let's just get through the day and night, and then we don't have to worry about it.*

I got up and took my time reaching the door while Luke waited patiently, looking at me through the glass pane with an annoyed look. "Any day now, Augusta," he said.

"Let's not fight, Luke," I said as I gave him a quick kiss on the lips. "I love you, and everything is going to be okay. It always is. Let's go for a drive and see some more of this beautiful countryside. I love all the old farms and reservoirs they have around here. Who knew all these lakes and state parks were even here? That just goes to show you that even though we both lived in Connecticut for years before we moved to Florida, we never really left our backyards or never thought we should or had a reason to. This experience alone will be perfect for me, honey, and you also. I will learn to be more independent like I know I am supposed to be, and you will learn to let go, which we both know you need to."

We spent the day riding around the back roads through the thick canopies of trees that draped over the winding back hill roads and stopped to look at the horses and cows in the many open fields and pastures that blanketed the vistas.

"Antique stores everywhere, Luke, and little country stores, and I love all the old churches and, wow, look at that barn! Amazing! Tell me you don't like it, Luke. Come on, and admit it. Oh my god! Is that a biker bar? Look at that, so many Harleys. There have to be hundreds of them. Let stop and go in and get a drink, honey. Can we? Can we? You might as well go in with me now because you know I will go in on my own after you leave anyway."

"Great, Augusta, now I have to worry about you coming here alone and drinking and driving home or hooking up with a bunch of lowlifes."

"Sincerely, Luke, you are calling them lowlifes? You do know how hilarious that sounds. They will most likely be moving and walking to the other side of the bar when you walk in. You do know that many people, if they did not get to know you, would think immediately you were a lowlife, right?"

"Okay, fine, stop laughing. I can't believe that came out of my mouth either. Let's have a drink and check this place out."

"Wow. What a cool place. Now this place looks like fun, but everyone is staring at us. Luke, they stare at us wherever we go because we look like such an unlikely pair. People get confused. You look like them, and I look like Mary Poppins today. I should have at least put on my jeans."

"Yes, Augusta, you do look like a Fairfield County high-maintenance goody two-shoes."

We quickly made friends and felt very comfortable. Luke was enjoying the attention he was getting from the sexy bartender with boobs I would kill to have. I did feel like a goody two-shoes dressed in the yuppie clothes I had on that day. Luke fit right in because he always wore and looked like a biker man and didn't own anything in the yuppie family. I knew this was just the ticket I needed to relax him and took advantage of his love for his bike and said, "I can see you here, Luke, pulling up on a Sunday afternoon with your Harley, can't you?" And in a teasing unthreatening tone, I added, "Of course I would have to make sure that bartender Becky over there was not working" loud enough for Becky to hear her.

"You had better believe it, girl," Becky said. "Your man is quite sexy, smiling at me. I would take real good care of him."

"Speaking of that, Becky, do me a favor. I have to go back to Florida tomorrow to take care of some business for a while, but Augusta is staying here and obviously will be back here. Don't let anything happen to her while I am gone, okay? Becky, would you do that for me?"

"Sure, sweetheart, we will take real good care of her. We are all like family here, and no one messes with our family right, right, Woody, Cowboy?"

"Right, Becky. Don't you worry, Luke. She is always safe if she is here. We will make sure of it."

The afternoon was perfect, and Luke was finally relaxed, and for the first time, he felt like maybe things would be okay. I knew the shot of tequila and two beers he had helped, but I would take anything I could get at that point.

Luke got up from the barstool. "Okay, guys, it was great meeting all of you. I will see you in a few months when I get back, and remember"—he laughed—"I will kick all your asses if you don't watch out for my wife while I am gone."

"You got it, Luke," the bartender said, "and you have a safe trip back."

The rest of the day and night was peaceful and uneventful. The house was quiet, and all the last-minute details that Luke felt he needed to accomplish and go over with me were completed. I was just going with the flow as I was used to Luke needing to be in control and overprotective. The house would be quiet until he left because I knew it had to be that way if he was going to leave at all.

"Are you going to miss me at all when I leave, Augusta? You probably can't wait until I get on that plane, and you are free. Am I right?"

He was right in a way, but yes, I was going to miss him, and yes, I was nervous about being alone. I had to face it—I had not been allowed to be independent of anyone for a very long time. My daughter was about two hours south of there as were many of my family members, so I was not wholly cut off, but they were far enough away to give me space and the time I needed to figure things out.

As the plane took off, I sat in the truck for a while, taking some deep breaths, composing myself before I hit the interstate back to the house—the house that was waiting for my return.

As I pulled into the driveway, a smile was on my face, and a sigh of relief relaxed my stiff muscles. The bush in the garden was in full bloom now with beautiful white flowers when earlier none were present. The smell of honeysuckles filled the air, and a breeze greeted me welcome home. I went around to the back of the house and up the four cement steps. The door opened slowly for me, just as it always did. The home was perfect, and the house cat that we had decided to name Porter (not knowing why) for the first time asked to enter the house and be with me.

"Okay, I am here now, house, and we are alone. Let's talk and get to know one another. Is there anything you need to tell me, and is there something you want from me, or do you have something for me?" I chuckled, not expecting to get any kind of reply or sign just because I asked, but I had to try. "Okay then, when you are ready. I am in no rush. I will be here for a long time by myself. The only thing I ask is, don't do anything to scare me, okay?"

I went about my business pitter-pattering around, jotting down all the items I needed, or just plain wanted to get for the house to make myself comfortable. What a great house this was and how comfortable and relaxed I felt until the evening came and everything was so hushed.

I knew I had to go to bed so that I could get up early in the morning to start to look for a job. I was not worried about it because everything was the way it was supposed to be; as long as I continued to let things just be, it would work out. The answers would show themselves to me if I just took the time to listen and recognize them and act on them when they revealed themselves. I knew that although it wasn't my first choice, I could just go back to being a waitress or bartender; that was fast money, and I was a natural at hospitality. Still, I wanted a job back in the hotel business, where I found the most enjoyment and where I could grow and make some real money someday if I stuck with it. The problem was that the only hotel, if that was what you wanted to call it, was the little Best Western down the street, where we stayed the very first night they arrived.

It was late in the evening when I finally went upstairs. I double-checked that all the doors were locked and all the windows were closed and secured. The cellar door was not only locked but also bolted, and a chair back was placed under the doorknob to make sure the bad from the cellar could not escape. I only had to walk by that door in the kitchen corner, and I would get a chill and a sense of unease. I left the light on over the kitchen sink just so there was a night-light available (note to self: buy some electrical wall-socket night-lights) and continued up the old wooden staircase to my small bedroom that was only big enough for my queen-sized bed and thin, tall dresser. No pictures hung on the wall, and there was no room for any side tables. The windows, though old with chipped paint, could be opened and screens put in, allowing the night breeze to flow. I stopped in the doorway, looking at the sparse room that seemed to belong in the seventeenth century. I smiled and thought, *Perfect.*

I lay flat on my back with my eyes closed and consciously breathed through my nose and out through my mouth to place myself into a deep sleep. I could hear the occasional vehicle go by on the road below my window. Then I heard voices. I found that strange as I could not fathom why anyone would be walking on the road this time of night. I realized the whispers were not coming from outside but from inside the house. I sprang up, sitting in bed, waiting for the next sound. *The voices are coming from the TV!*

I knew I had turned it off, and so it began. I had to address this issue head-on right away, and I could not and would not let whoever or whatever was occupying the house with me scare or control me. I was supposed to be there, and I was staying, and even though they were there first, they had to learn to share and behave.

I took a deep breath and yelled out, "Okay! You have let me know you are here, and I understand you want something or need something from me. Talk to me. Show yourself to me."

There was a bang, and the definitive sound of furniture being dragged across the wooden floor. The TV volume increased, cabinet doors slammed, and I heard distinctive giggling that was barely audible over the now-blaring

TV noise. I wasn't afraid; I was annoyed. I jumped out of bed and stomped down the staircase. I stood in the middle of the living room and screamed louder than the TV, "Stop it! Stop it now!"

To my surprise, the TV shut down, and the only sound left was a few of the cabinet doors going back to their original closed position with a little click.

"Thank you, we need to talk about this. I am here. I am not going anywhere, and I am not sure if it has been you all these years haunting me to come here, nor do I yet know why. If it is, we need to learn how to coexist. We need to learn to communicate. Right now, you need to be quiet and allow me to sleep. Leave all the furniture you have misplaced where it is, and I will put it back myself in the morning. Okay? Okay, good night."

I fell into a deep sleep—no dreams and no disturbing noises for the remainder of the night. I made it through my first night alone in our place. I snickered to myself, *Well, maybe not completely alone.* It was fresh for a June morning, unlike Florida, where 6:00 AM brought seventy-five- to eighty-degree temperatures. I felt good and alive and happy and could not wait to start my day.

It was Monday morning—no work to hurry to, no husband to cook for, and no animals to feed. *Wow, I am not used to this, but for a while, I think I am going to love it.* I put on a CD of Native American music. Flutes, drums, chanting, and wildlife sounds filled the house. Not sure why this seemed to be the music of choice that morning. Now I had to put back all the chairs currently residing in the kitchen back in the dining room—compliments of my friend or friends last night—and push back the couch and loveseat to their proper positions. I drank my coffee and pitter-pattered around most of the morning, emptying boxes and decorating the house with a few items I brought with me. I knew the number one item on my list was to find a job.

To do that, I had to set up my desktop computer. Where to do that was the next question. We have two unused rooms upstairs, so which one would it be? Entering the second bedroom, I stood there and closed my eyes for a moment to see if I could envision myself spending a lot of time in that room working on the computer. There was a lovely window that overlooked the reservoir and a perfect place for my little antique desk though the room had only one outlet, and that was on the opposite wall. No view there.

The hair on the back of my neck and arms was starting to stand up like a faint electrical current was going through me. I shivered with the sensation, but I cannot say I was cold, just not right. I felt nausea and buckled over with a sudden stomach cramp; the shivering turned to wet clammy sweat. *No, I do not like this room.*

I did not like it when I first entered it days before, and I didn't like it now. I did not see myself spending any extended time in here, so the little closet room it was. *I will make that room work as a wardrobe closet and a workstation.*

It took me much of the afternoon to set up the computer and get it connected to the Internet, which was connected to AOL. What would we do without computers and the Internet? I knew if I could not get the connection to work, I would have to go to the general store down the street and purchase the local newspaper want ads. I also realized that most bartender/waitress jobs would not be online, so picking up a paper would be a good idea. I could stop in the little B&B inn on my way and find out if they might be looking for some help or if they could refer me to another hotel or inn for employment.

The little lodge had nothing available being a family-run operation with all positions filled by siblings, cousins, and spouses. They had no recommendations for me unless I wanted to travel to Hartford, which was at least an hour away. I hated city life, and it made me nervous, just thinking about going and working in a big city. There were numerous job postings for wait staff, but this area was rural with farms and farmer-type people. Hence, the only local restaurants were establishments like Friendly's, McDonald's, Chuck E. Cheese, a local dinner, and a lot of pizza pubs. There was one advertisement with an excellent dining restaurant food server wanted. It was called the Railroad Restaurant, and it was somewhere in Stone, Connecticut. The ad said to apply in person. It was already 3:00 PM, so it would be the very first thing I would do the next day. I wanted to go home and see if I could get my computer working so that I could type up a résumé highlighting my skills directed at being a food server. I had a résumé so far for the possible hotel positions, one for retail stores, one for essential office work, and now I would make one for the restaurant business.

I wanted to get home now. I needed to get back for some reason and smiled when I pulled into the driveway. I had left the computer running while I was gone so it might connect itself and do whatever it needed to do while I was completing my errands. Yes, it seemed to be connected now, so I could begin to work. I would be fine as long as someone did not call me because then I would be disconnected; after all, the phone line was my computer line.

Just as I was saving my updated restaurant résumé, the phone rang, and just like that, my connection dropped. It was Luke, upset because I had not called him first thing in the morning or all afternoon. He was frantic, and his imagination had run amuck. I let him rant and rave for a while and realized if the shoe was on the other foot, I might feel the same way. I felt terrible that it did not even occur to me that I should have phoned him before I started my day, and he was trying to give me my space and waited as long as he could before he called me. After he got it all out and apologized for being a maniac, he asked all the obvious questions, and we talked for about a half hour.

The house was surprisingly quiet, and I knew I wanted to start up communication again, but I had to concentrate on finding employment first. Just like Luke, the house was giving me space and time I needed.

The restaurant manager was a little surprised when I turned up to apply in person with a résumé in hand. He said no one had ever done that. I got the job but had a lot of training to do as an excellent dining service is a lot different from a typical restaurant. I was to start training in two days, so I would be ready to rock and roll when the university summer conference attendees began to arrive in mid-June. It wasn't my dream work by any means, but it was a start, and I was grateful for the opportunity.

Now that I had managed to find a job in only three days, I was feeling quite good about myself and ready to concentrate on the house and my invisible but boisterous roommates. I wonder if Luke would be happy I found employment or not so much because, down deep, he wanted me to fail.

Driving home, I decided to take a ride through this university campus. I never went to college but had worked at the community college in Florida during my recovery and reeducation and had a very high opinion of the educational system. The campus was massive, and I was only exploring the main roads; there were many side roads that I saved for another day. It was summer break, but when school was not in session, the campus became one significant conference destination. In place of young adults, I saw middle-aged business people from every walk of life. My favorite place was the sign that said HORSE ROLLING HILL ROAD.

There were horses everywhere and huge massive barns fenced and cross-fenced with white vinyl. Horse Rolling Hill Road was the agricultural section of the university. These were the hills and pastures I had seen in my visions, breathtaking as far as the eye could see. I had to pull my car off the side of the twisting road because my view became blurred with tears of joy. I couldn't explain to anyone what it felt like to see dreams become a reality.

I could not wait to call Luke and tell him about my day. I had left the computer running because it took so long to warm up—just in case I needed to jump on the Internet again. I sat down at my desk to disconnect and make my phone call. There was an advertisement popping up in the center of the screen, and a work ad, a rendered sketch of a hotel called the Stone Hotel. "University campus, group salesperson wanted. Send résumé." Wow! I had chills up my spine. I have a new dream job! I knew it was mine; I just had to go through the motions. Luke's phone call would have to wait; I was jumping on this one immediately.

It took me about an hour to tweak my hotel résumé to make it sound perfect for this particular position, and I sent it off. The phone rang, and it was Luke again, trying not to seem too annoyed with me once again for not being the one to call. I was so excited that he had to reel my excitement in to slow me down so I could give him a recap of my day's events. He was surprisingly supportive and seemed generally happy for me. What a day! I was curious how long it would be before someone called me to set up an interview.

I found myself sitting in the living room, drinking a hot cup of tea and talking. Who was I talking to? Was I having a conversation with myself or with someone? I must have blacked out or maybe dozed off and only thought I had a conversation. Anyway, either I was an excellent listener or my invisible roommate was. When I last looked, it was only 7:30 PM, and it was now 10:00 PM. I had lost hours, and my bed was calling me.

I staggered up the stairs toward my bedroom. Straight ahead was the awful pink bathroom. I noticed the pop-in screen in the bathroom was crooked and dislodged and about to fall out. I went to fix it, and no sooner did I enter the bathroom than the little square screen flew out of the window outside down onto the front-door steps. Damn, that was weird. *I better get it and pray it isn't bent or broken. I wonder why that happened.*

I opened the front door, stepped out onto the landing, picked up the little screen, and turned to reenter the house. There in the door was my key ring still lodged in the door lock. Oh no! When I came home today, my hands were full, and it was easier for me to go in through the front door, which I usually never do. I forgot to take the keys out of the door, and they had been there all day. It was a good thing that I came down to look because the keyring had a night-light that came on automatically when it was dark so they are easy to find. It would have been a beacon that the keys were there for anyone walking or driving by. I was a little taken aback but thanked the house for making me look.

My bed was now quite comfortable, and the fresh air flowing through the window encouraged me to pull up the folded light comforter on the bottom. I fell into a deep sleep and dreamed about a time long ago. I was never good at history, so I didn't know what year it might have been, but I was among a Native American tribe walking through the field that was still behind the house. The area was now full of cornrows and people tending the stalks. I noticed many of the women entering the wooded area southeast of the field. They had children in tow carrying baskets, and I believed they had some sort of fishing lines. I wanted to pursue them, but I was startled by the horn of a truck driving down the street. I glanced over at the little travel clock I had on the dresser, and it was 6:00 AM.

I was excited to start a new day. I had this one day free before I had to start training at the Railroad Restaurant, the employment I would keep until my hotel job came through. I knew I was going to get that interview, and the job eventually, but I never put all my eggs in one basket as I had learned not to do over my years of experience—anything can happen.

As I stood at the kitchen sink looking out at the backfield, I remembered my dream. I had not given much thought to the wooded area before, and now I had to investigate. I recalled the women carrying baskets loaded with corn and vegetables and felt I should do the same thing. I had a little straw basket on the top of the refrigerator, corn that I had just brought from the market, and an overripe tomato that was a little too squishy for me.

I put on my hiking boots, long pants, and long sleeves as the field might have things like snakes and deer ticks. It was a longer walk than I thought and was already quite warm for 7:00 AM. As I got closer to the woods, I thought I saw someone standing in the shadows of the trees, but when I looked closer, he/she was gone.

What a beautiful place. The trees consisted of evergreens, maples, and oak, and though it was very dense, the ground was surprisingly clear for walking. More rooted in the forest were several large rocks that looked misplaced as they protruded from the ground. I was frozen with a vision from back in time.

I could see women and children praying over loved ones' graves and leaving food at the base of each stone. There was no large reservoir at this time but a large wide running river. One child seemed to notice me and tugged on her mother's dress, pointing in my direction. The women did not see what the child saw and handed then an ear of corn to place on the ground, distracting them from the apparition of me. I was back in real time now and knew the large stones were gravestones and the food was a gift for their loved ones who had passed. On the far side of the forest, there was a small cleared area on the banks of the reservoir. Someone, if they had a fishing pole, could relax and catch their next meal. I had to assume the lake was added sometime in later years as it was not there originally. I placed my food offering next to one of the stones and proceeded back to the house. I felt so blessed.

It was time to visit the attic. The third floor was vast and would have to be a storage area for my store-bought temporary wardrobe closets until I could convert that shoebox of a room into a closet/computer room. I proceeded to go up the stairway to the attic space. It was so narrow that one almost had to turn sideways to ascend. I was hoping to find some treasures that had been left behind, but there were none. The place was empty—not even an old metal clothes hanger or Christmas ornament. It was very steamy and hot up there, so I would not be able to store anything that might melt in the heat, but it had possibilities. I turned to go down the stairs and realized I had to descend the way one would go down a ladder; it was too steep and too narrow to walk straight down.

BANG!

What was that? It sounded like a board broke up here. I better find out where so that I can add it to the list of things that the not-yet-hired carpenter needs to fix. I scanned the room, looking in the rafters' walls and corners and noticed that to the right of the stairs was a piece of wood that was protruding. It was still being held in place on each end but buckled in the middle. By its age, it looked original to the house. Each end of the boards was fixed firmly to the frame of the floor. Removing it wasn't an option unless I had a hammer and gloves, but the bend was big enough for someone's intent and sufficient to push a hand down into the opening and feel around. My guts told me there was something there and to go for it, but my stomach said no! *Gloves and hammer please, let's not be stupid.*

My phone was ringing in the kitchen two floors down. I had taken it off the base in the office earlier, so it was convenient when I was not in the office. There was no way I could get to it in time, and I knew it was the call I was hoping to get. I did try though, but after the sixth ring, it went silent. *Fuck! Well, if it was something important, they will leave a message,* I thought as I caught my breath. I waited and heard the ding. "You have received a new message."

"Hi, this is Susan. I am calling about the résumé you sent applying for the group sales position. I would like to meet and talk further. Please give me a callback, and we can set up a day and time."

I checked my restaurant training schedule and called Susan with dates and times that would work. We decided to meet at a Friendly's ice cream parlor located across the street from the main campus entrance.

The hotel under construction would be called the Stone Hotel and was located on the university campus. It was privately owned but would be run by a management firm, and that firm would hire me. Construction on the building had started, and the doors were scheduled to open in about a year. They wanted to place people in key positions to support the hotel and get it all up and running in the back office. Reservations would be taken on paper and then inputted into a reservation system once it was ready.

Susan thought I was perfect for the job and liked the fact that I lived only one mile from the office, had just purchased a house, and currently lived alone as the job was going to be demanding, with extended hours. The campus was a learning place, and I would eventually be teaching the students hotel management as well as explaining and instructing some of the university staff how to put on a conference. The main objective, of course, was putting heads in beds. I was to start on July 1.

There it was, the next prediction. "You will go to a learning place and work among the children." I guess they would be children to me as they were at least fifteen to twenty years younger than me.

I continued to decorate the house and acknowledge my unseen roommates. Everything was as good as it could be. I was into my second week working at the restaurant, developing my fine-dining skills, and making enough money to keep my head above water, knowing my real paying job was only a few weeks away.

I was running late one day and was scrambling to organize myself before leaving for work. I had the curling iron for my hair, the dryer running for my uniform black pants, and I was in a panic because I could not find my black bowtie. I had to leave my breakfast dishes in the sink for washing later. I grabbed my car keys and headed out the back door around to the front of the house to the driveway. I heard a loud bang as I passed the downstairs bathroom window. What was that? I ran back to the already-opened back door.

The small wooden shelf that I put up myself above the toilet had fallen, scattering and breaking the items that I had placed on it. What a mess it made, but it was going to have to wait until I got home because I was already so late. I was just about to leave when I smelled something burning. I had left my hair curling iron on, and it was leaning up again a roll of toilet paper sitting on the corner of the bathroom basin. It was ready to catch fire! *Wow, I could have burned down the house. I am such an idiot and so lucky that the shelf fell, and I came back. Or was it? Okay, okay, I know. Thank you. I will be more careful. I get the message.*

I tried to talk to Luke every day, but most of the time, our connection was full of static, and though he could hear me, I was not always able to listen to what he was saying to me. We assumed maybe it was because the computer and phone lines were connected, and it would be a good idea when I was making some steady money to get a second line. He was making plans to come for a visit in September, and this time, he was going to bring the dog to stay with me. I knew I had resentment residing deep inside regarding Luke and his refusal, or maybe his denial, of many of the reasons why indeed I was there. He had not even placed the Florida house on the market yet. It was not just because I finally found the home; there was a lot more to it than that. I needed to get away from him and the life he had decided was right for me. It was something I had to do and he refused to see. He wanted us to live in a world he built around his comfort zone. He wanted his children to stay sweet and innocent, and he could never believe they were capable of tormenting me the way they had for years. He never wanted to admit that I had gifts that I planned on using, and he was mad (understandably) that I was peculiar. He knew I was not nuts because he had experienced many events that were called paranormal.

I was glad he was coming for a visit, but I knew that was all it was. He was not yet ready to give up the life he had built in Florida surrounded by all the familiar people and things that made him comfortable to be with me, the new me, the one he was not sure about in a house that scared the hell out of him. I tried to be more understanding because I knew it was a lot for him to handle. He had always hated change, and that was what he had to face every day with me, a continually changing world. He felt I was trying to force him into transition. I did not want to push him. I wanted him to choose for himself, and if he decided to stay where he was, doing that was right for him but not for me. Trying to make it more difficult for me in subtle ways of manipulation was making it harder for me to succeed, and that was unacceptable. I was glad it was just a visit. I was angry with him whether I had a right to be or not.

I went to bed and lay there, asking for guidance. In my dream state, I was welcomed by a distinguished man with dark eyes and white hair and a full beard. I had seen him before. He was the one who held and comforted me the night I had that awful dream of being led to my death in a wagon surrounded by others who had the same fate as I did. "Who are you? Why are you here? Will you tell me why I am here?"

"My name is Jonathan, and I am here for you. I have always been with you. You will remember when you are ready. I was with you in this lifetime when you were a small child and wanted to explore. I was with you every time you decided to travel on your own, walking down the hall toward the light, not knowing what door to open or if you should continue past all the entries. I have helped you find this journey here, and I have made it possible for you to be here alone for as long as needed so that you can find the knowledge you seek and have been looking for so long. You know you are not just merely a product of fate, right? You know you have a purpose. You have lived on this earth—I call it this plane—many, many times, but this time you have fought harder and come further, arriving at this point. Every life you have lived, every door in the past you have opened was so that you could gather knowledge, experience many lifetimes to see different faces and creeds, and to accept many different religions. There are many of us here with you. Some are here to keep you safe and help you through this part of your journey, and some are here to stop you, to instill fear and even end this journey if they can. You will identify the mysteries of all time that is you."

"I have so many questions: Why were my memories taken away from me?"

"Because, Augusta, everything you are you have become over many lifetimes, not just this one. The experiences and memories of your life have not been stolen from you. You've agreed to let them go. Your memories were a deterrent, closing your mind to other possibilities, and you volunteered to shed them so that you could be reborn into this same vessel instead of the alternative. It was a faster route to your destination and a small price to pay. That is why we—you—put people and experiences in place to help you and why you let all others go."

Chapter 12

Reincarnation

"Who was I before? What were my other lives? Why here and why now?" I asked.

"There are many places on this earth where the energy fields are stronger, where energy seeks out different energy looking for connections," Jonathan replied. "This house, this place, is ancient and is one of those magnets. You've been attracted to this place and it to you. Here, you will feel the forbidden and the knowledge of your latent skills. Everyone has the same abilities inside of them. Still, they have no idea because those entities have chosen a more earth-grounded path, one of comfort and acceptance. You, on the other hand, searched and found another possibility and are willing to pay the price. Who you were in past lives makes no difference because when you leave one life, you go on to a greater one. You advance. You are sent back or choose to come back here to continue learning. You do not have to go back, but you have chosen to because the learning and the experiences you acquire every time you do helps you reach that final destination you believe you want but are still not ready to accept. Reincarnation is truth, and it is merely giving up your body for a new one because whatever attitude you had at that time permits it."

"So we are doomed to just go on and on in a circle, Jonathan? Is there no end?"

"Of course, there is an end if you choose it to be so. It is one's attitude toward life that allows its cycles, and it only seems circular. No one forces you to come back here, but after an eon of living on this planet, humans begin to think that that is all there is. You have to be ready and willing to let go and continue to another plane. If you are looking for someone to blame for all the confusion, pain, and suffering you have experienced in this life, look no further than a mirror. You are who you are right now because you were all the others before. You are not that starving person on the wagon going to your death because you already have been that suffering soul. You are not the young man fighting in one of the world wars because you have already done that, and you have already been the baker, and now you have chosen to be the person who buys from the baker."

Getting to Know My Surroundings

What a dream! Is it morning already? Did I sleep? I feel like I slept. Time to start a new day. Maybe I will venture into the basement today. If Jonathan is correct, I will be encountering many more apparitions, some good and some bad. I know some of that bad is in two places in this house, down in the basement for sure, and something is not right in the second bedroom upstairs. I feel invincible today, time to kick some boogeyman ass. If these spirits are here because of me, I am going to be in charge. If they are kind, they can stay. If I encounter some that are not, they must leave.

I fearlessly unbolted the cellar door, turned the knob, and reached into the dark, feeling for the light switch against the wire-exposed wall, just waiting for something to grab my hand and toss me down the cobwebby stairs to the cold basement floor. Okay, all good so far; nothing like that happened. I reached the bottom step, stopped, looked around at the intimidating damp, musty room. Except for the water heater, the boiler, some old paint cans, and a few canning jars scattered about, the place was empty. I looked over the space, and my eyes drifted to a section of the floor raised toward the back of the room; the remains of coal were spread all over the black earth, emanating a sweet, musty scent. Something told me that more than fuel was once stored there. I decided to take an alpha stand on the chance a not-so-friendly spirit resided here. I mustered up a stern voice and said, "You are only here because of me. You are the anger in me and the revenge that sits on the sidelines, and if you intend any harm to me or anyone I love, I will banish you, so remember that!"

Just as I was feeling quite proud of myself and a little cocky, a wave of nausea came over me. My ears started to ring, and I went into a cold sweat. *Okay, well, I guess I just pissed them off—time to retreat and rebolt the door.*

It had been enough for one day. The second bedroom was going to have to wait. I had to get back to my mental health. I often went to the wooded area, always bringing peace offerings with me. I even spent time by the reservoir's edge, catching an occasional meal. I was pleased and lucky to find this spot by the side of the water hidden from prying eyes.

I started my new job, and I loved it. It kept me busy and focused during the day, always happy and eager to return home. I just placed my pocketbook on the kitchen island, getting ready to make my nightly call to Luke when there was a knock on the front door.

There stood a police officer looking around his surroundings. I opened the door slowly and said, "Yes, can I help you? Hello, Officer. Is there something wrong?"

"No, he said not at all. I just wanted to welcome you to the neighborhood. I have noticed you've been here for about a month now. I've been wondering how things are going. Is everything okay?"

"Yes, thank you, should I be concerned about something?"

"No, I just wanted to meet the person who could stay in this house for more than one week. Most leave by now."

"How rude of me," I answered. "Would you like to come in and have a drink and talk?" His police car was in the driveway. He had a badge and helpful eyes, so I felt safe inviting him in.

"Thank you. You work at the hotel on the university campus, correct? The word around campus is that the house has found a friend, so that must be you. The house has been rented on and off over the years, being so close to the campus. I have been called out here on several occasions because of disturbances. I never found anything to report, so no need for you to be worried. I did notice you walking into the woods last Sunday with a basket and fishing pole though."

"Yes, that was me. Am I in trouble? I see the sign that states no entry, private property. I know I am not supposed to use the reservoir."

"Not at all, the flag is to keep people out, but you live here, so as long as you are respectful, I do not have a problem with it. I have tried to go fishing in there several times myself over the years, but something would always push me away, knock me down, and trip me. I don't think I am welcomed in there like you are. Have you experienced any of that?"

"No, Officer, I find it very peaceful in the woods and sitting by the edge of the water. I do bring gifts for the spirits that occupy the area though every time I go. I believe it is an ancient Native American burial ground."

"Wow, I am impressed you know that. There are only a few of us on the board of the historical society who know that. The field and woods are city-owned lands. We want to keep it quiet so the state doesn't come in and take over. We are a close small community, and we would like certain things kept low-key. I guess what I am asking is now knowing that you will be visiting the woods on occasion, would you please not mention anything to the locals or your university colleagues about what you think you have found? I wanted to give you my direct telephone number in case you wanted or needed to reach me. I am glad you are here and like the place. This house needs someone to look after it. It is part of our oldest historical homes here in Stone." The officer extended his hand, saying goodbye, and stated, "I like what you have done to the place. Welcome to the neighborhood."

I was pleased that I made a friend who was looking out for me and was okay with me bending the rules. I was relieved I could go into the woods without worrying that I was going to get into trouble.

I continued to go with the flow. The odd occurrences in the house became the new norm. I went to work and came home to gardens that seemed to take care of themselves and doors that would open and close for me. The cat would be gone all day and enter at night, and life was good.

I was making my way back up to the attic with gloves, hammer, and flashlight in hand this time. I was eager now to find out if there was something for me to find under that dislodged floorboard. The idea was to try to spend some time in the second bedroom coming down from the attic. To reach the attic, one had to go through the second bedroom, so I sprinted across the floor to the narrow staircase. I felt a sadness come over me as soon as I entered that bedroom, but it gave way to a playful happy feeling once I reached the top landing leading to the attic floor. Placing the gloves on my hands, I was able to maneuver the flashlight inside the hole without having to pry up the loose board. I started to feel around and felt a small container move to one side. It was not of significant size, and I was able to grab it and, not without difficulty, slip it out of the floor opening.

The box was a small ancient wooden box, and it looked handmade. I was thrilled and anxious to see its contents. Within there was a tiny ring encrusted with an antique pearl—the stone's once-exquisite color had been dulled by dust, dirt, and years of neglect. There was a pink ribbon and playhouse-sized doll that looked handmade and a handkerchief with the initials *SP* embroidered on the right corner. *What a great find!*

I knew not to take the items away from their home. I placed the box and contents on the floor next to the hole and left it there for SP to find. I turned to back down the attic stairs and felt a soft brush against my cheek, and I knew I did right.

As soon as my foot hit the floor of the second bedroom, an overwhelming sadness filled me again. Tears filled my eyes. I wanted to help and had no idea how. Evil did not fill this room; it was filled with grief, pain, loneliness, and helplessness.

Chapter 13

Levels

Every night I would visit with Jonathan, and he would teach me so many things and answered so many of my questions. I asked about the second bedroom, and what I felt encompassing those four walls.

"Jonathan, can you give me knowledge of the sadness there?"

"Yes, there are different levels of planes and consciousness. Each level vibrates on a different frequency. I will just touch on this explanation because you would need to experience these planes yourself to understand the depth involved. Some people like yourself can sense these other-level vibrations. You see some of them in a light form or auras of color because they are vibrating on a level different from yours. As you understand, accept, and embrace what you are feeling, these energies that reside on these various planes can communicate with you—especially the ones that are on the second level."

"There are *seven levels* of existence. Life never ends. Only the physical body ends, and once the soul leaves the body, it turns into light or a form of energy. That person's thoughts and instilled beliefs at the time of physical death determine which plane—level—they accept.

"*Level one* is the plane you exist on now. You perceive it as three dimensional. This earth level is where entities gain knowledge and fundamental truth and an understanding of God in the form of matter. You are born in the flesh, and it can be a struggle as you have to grow within the limitations of flesh. Coming back to the first plane is the fastest way to achieve a new thought process. That is not the only reason people keep coming back though they come back because they have lived many lives here and have high emotional attachments. It is home to them.

"*Level two* is like a state of consciousness that is flat. The explanation of level two is long because it is the level you will understand the most. There are thousands of spirits there and some of the ones you will feel in this house. You feel sad in that room. Your light awakened one of the entities residing on the second level, and your presence woke them from their slumber. They recognize the strength of the energy light that emanates from you—the residual imprint from the time you died physically. Souls on this second level were told that when they died, they had to wait for the Messiah to come back and bring them home to heaven. If on their death they believed they were worthy and pure, they were allowed to go straight to heaven. I think the Bible calls these levels limbo and purgatory.

"There are so many souls on this level waiting for their resurrection, waiting for a light to save them. Some get confused when they see an energy light like yours that is grander and brighter than theirs, and they think you are their messiah. They wake up so you can help and guide them. The others stay in slumber because they were taught and believed that when they died, the devil would try to trick them and tempt them to arise to a false messiah, and then they would be lost forever. Those who refuse to wake up will stay that way until higher-level energy—known in the Bible as Jesus, the Son of God—wakes them up. They think they only have to wait. They don't have to wait, and you can help some of the levels two entities pass on because you can wake them. They are sad and confused but are trying to communicate and willing to accept your help.

"There is a level-two entity in that room you speak of trying to communicate. You feel sadness but not anger in that room. The ones you have to worry about, the ones who are a threat to you and your loved ones, also reside on level two, but it is a *sublevel of level two*, a place inside a level. These spirits do not believe there is life after death. They live in an area of pain. I think the Bible refers to this as hell, pure evil, and the devil. All the other plains have hope and are majestic. These entities are stuck in this sublevel place because their souls were so bound to their physical bodies, material things, power, greed, and the need to be worshipped. This was the most essential thing in their lives. Anything else was too terrifying for them to consider as a possibility. In human life, they felt superior to all others. They would cause conflict and start wars to instill fear so that the masses would believe and follow them. They found these things to be the absolute truth, so it had become their reality when it was time for them to shed their bodies. They know they are no longer part of the plane you occupy, but they want to be. They want your energy, to feel what you feel, to instill fear if they must to get it. They still want to be in control. They want to move on but don't know how, and just as in life, they resort to their destructive ways to get what they want. They will do anything to have it. If they can learn and evolve from this sublevel, they will most likely go to the third plane, which is one of power. Here, they experience grief, remorse, and guilt, which are a step up from where they were. Reaching plane three allows them to learn if they can stop trying to control and enslave others, trying to get everyone to see their point of view.

"*Level three* is the most beautiful level where green grass, majestic mountains, flowers, and crystal-bright aqua-blue water welcomes you. You have visited this plane, Augusta, in your childhood travels. I was with you because you asked me to take you several times. The third plane is one of love. There, one can feel very deeply but unfortunately cannot express it, so they usually decide to return to plane one to learn how to express love.

"*Level four* is grander as love is felt and expressed. It is a very peaceful place to be, and plane five's light is visible and shines brighter and higher and calls them. Most do not stay on plane four for long.

"*Level five* is paradise. Many are very happy there and never want to leave because they can't imagine that there is any place grander than this one. Resting, they ponder why they deserve to be in such a beautiful place. They begin to see additional lights. These lights are no brighter or less critical than their own. All of the lights resonate together. As soon as they comprehend this awareness, they move on to the sixth level. They know everything is one, and now they understand.

"*Level six* is the plane of understanding. Heaven and I have no words to explain it other than you see. You are one with everything and everyone. Level six is the gateway.

"*Level seven* is the pure God, pure light, total knowing. On this level, you know you are one with God. The seventh level is where everyone eventually wants to be. You will know God when you know yourself.

"Augusta, I have told you a lot. There is a lot to absorb. I will leave you alone now so that you can contemplate all I have said. If you decide to learn more, I will help you to proceed."

Chapter 14

Luke's First Visit

I was busy with my new job and making new friends. I was amazed when it was September already, and Luke and Muggsy, our Great Dane, were on their way up for a visit. Luke rented a car with Muggsy in tow and assumed it would take two days of travel. It was Sunday, so no work. I thought, *He is going to be tired when he gets here. I will make an excellent supper.*

Muggsy jumped out of the car and greeted me with pure love. Luke looked exhausted and hungry. We settled in for the night because he arrived later than expected.

It was weird sharing my bed with someone after having the whole thing to myself for three and a half months. The evening was quiet; no incidents occurred, thank goodness, and we discussed what Luke wanted to accomplish during his two-week visit. As we held each other while drifting off to sleep, Luke started to have a panic attack; he sat up in bed, clutching his chest, yelling, "I can't breathe!"

I tried to talk him down, rubbing his back, reassuring him everything was okay. Once he got control of the situation, he said, "I don't like this room. It feels like someone is sitting on my chest."

I tried to convince him it was because he was in a new place, and he did not do change well, but that only made him angry and misunderstood.

"I'm here only one night, and this house is already letting me know that I'm not welcome. I am going to sleep on the couch, and maybe they will leave me alone. We need to get this house exorcised, and the sooner, the better."

This beginning was a disappointment, but I have to say that I was not surprised that his presence would be considered a threat. I wanted to tell him the information I received from my spiritual guide, Jonathan, but I was still processing it myself. I was in no way ready to teach it to someone else, especially to someone with a mind closed to enlightenment. It took Luke a long time to somewhat accept my visions and paranormal gifts. There was no way he would be ready for this.

Luke was already up and moving around the kitchen, making coffee and eggs for me because I had to get to work. I was a little worried about leaving him home all alone, but there was nothing I could do, and the house had to accept him as a friend, not a threat. Luke gazed out the kitchen window that faced the field and water and took a big breath. "Wow, that is beautiful. Are there things you need doing in the house that is a priority other than the obvious like hanging curtain rods and moving unpacked boxes up into the attic? Can I see your list? You always have a honey-do list.

"While I am here, I would like to give that barn a good look, so we can decide if we can bring your horse, Sonny, here. I need to know it is safe for you and him. I have to agree that you're staying because you've got a fantastic job and you seem happy. I have to demand that we have someone here to deal with the *ghosts*! If I am going to stay here, they have to go. God, Augusta, do you like to be tormented this way?"

"Of course not, I have not been tormented, Luke. I don't fight them. You must stop fighting them and accept coexistence. I want you to be happy here and move in soon, but you have to admit what is going on here without the sinister outlook you have. You believe but not really. I can't protect you if you don't open your mind to all the possible reasons for what is going on in this house. If the word *haunted* works for you, then okay. I have to go to work, but enjoy your day and call me if you feel the need."

I worked through the day with no phone calls from Luke. That was a good sign or not. On my way home, I hoped and prayed all went well and I would find Luke working around the house and not huddled in the corner of some room or something worse.

I found him replacing the locks on all the exterior doors of the house. "Hey, may I ask what you are doing and why?"

"Well, Augusta, this house locked me out twice today. I had to climb through the kitchen window once, which was not an easy task even for a young person, and through the dining room window the second time. I have installed new locks that all work with the same key. I have placed a spare key in the shed. These sons of bitches are not going to keep me out."

"That is a brilliant move, Luke, and a great idea. We can talk about everything over dinner. I am so happy that you have decided to move up here soon. I have a lot to explain to you if you are willing to be open-minded enough to hear me out."

We sat and talked for hours into the night. I did most of the talking, watching Luke's facial expressions of doubt and amusement.

"So tell me, Augusta, this Jonathan person, is he a dirty dead older man that is obsessed with you? Do I have to worry about you cheating on me with a ghost?" Luke laughed and snickered.

"Hilarious, Luke, Jonathan is my protector and my guide. I told you there is positive and negative energy in this house, and if I run into a negative one that is strong and means you or me harm, Jonathan will help protect me from it. I am sure he would defend you also if I asked him to, but you have to believe before he can or will protect you."

"Okay, this is a little too far out for me to handle right now. I know you are entirely comfortable with this realm of reality, but you have had your whole life to understand and deal with it, and it is very new to me and hard to swallow. I will try to deal with what is going on, and I will even try to verbally project my intentions here and ask them to live with it. Will that make you happy for now? When I come to live here for good though if this shit is still happening, I will get them removed anyway I have to."

Oh, I thought to myself. I so wished he had not said that out loud while in the house. I had a feeling this journey for Luke will prove to be a long difficult one.

Before retiring for the night, I asked Luke to stand in the middle of the living room and speak directly to the entities of the house. He asked me to leave because he felt stupid doing it, but he would abide by the rules if I thought it would help. I don't know if he was talking to them that night or just humoring me, but I told him the first steps that I thought it was essential to do, and it was up to him to try. If Luke did work toward communicating with the entities that night, it did not work for him very well as the attacks were revving up.

We discussed hiring a local carpenter to fix the barn stairs and frame out the stalls, making it safer for my horse when he came. When several window panes slammed down just missing Luke's hands, he said the windows needed replacing. When he stubbed his toes several times when walking through the house or fell or was slammed into walls, he suggested that the floors were uneven and the boards required sanding. He insisted that the kitchen counters in the house were slanted when dishes and glasses would suddenly fall and smash onto the floor, once inflicting a large gash in his leg from the flying debris. He finally asked me if I, too, was seeing people in my peripheral vision as he was. I did not want to tell him that I saw much more than side visions but thought that would just be cruel.

"Augusta, God, I hate leaving you here alone, more so now than last time. I am going to place the Florida house on the market as soon as I get back. It is going to take a while to sell it, so I will plan to come back to visit again in a few months. The doggy door is in, so Muggsy can go in and out, and the underground electric fencing is working, so he has free rein to protect the house. Next time I come, we're going to set up at least a paddock area for Sonny so that we can transport him here. You're going to have your horse as well. I hope he will be here by February or March. Happy?"

I kissed Luke goodbye and watched him enter the terminal for as long as the airport authorities allowed me to sit in the drop-off lane.

Will You Stay? No One Ever Comes Back

I was thrilled to hear from my daughter whom I had not seen for a few months because of my new job and her new life with a baby. I was lonely for the family as Luke had not returned in a few months as he said he would, and I felt put out and angry with him. It made it all better when my daughter asked me if she and my grandson could come for a visit. I had suggested Friday through Sunday, but Tabitha wanted to come that day and did not know how long they would be staying. I told her she could stay forever if she wanted. I got a distinct feeling Tabitha needed space away from the baby's daddy.

I left a key for her under the back doormat and told her I would be home from work a few hours after she arrived. She asked me if she and the baby would be all right there alone because she had heard things. I told her, "Of course, don't be silly. You and the baby would be fine. The dog know you and loves babies."

She said, "Mom, you know that's not exactly what I'm saying."

We talked about her life over dinner and drinks. She was confused and wanted to vent about her living situation with the baby's daddy. He was a wonderful man and great father, but she was not in love with him and thought she was going to move in with some other single moms and try to make it on her own, but she did not have a good-paying job and did not know how she would pay for childcare and just thought maybe she should just stay with the father. I reassured her they could stay with me as long as they wanted, and we would figure it all out together. I told her not to worry; it was going to be fine as long as she believed it was going to be.

I did see her eyes roll as she said to me, "You and your positive attitude, this is the real world—it doesn't work that way for anybody but you."

Tabitha wanted to sleep on the pull-out couch in the living room as the second bedroom was too cold for her and the baby. I promised her that if they'd decided to move in, I'd get that fixed.

I went to work the next morning, giving suggestions and possible places for her to go to familiarize herself with the area. She insisted she would be just fine staying home with the baby as she needed to decompress from life.

It was just about time to shut down another workday, and I was packed up and ready to run home to my two house guests when Susan popped her head into my office and said, "Augusta, the front desk received a phone call from your daughter. She sounded upset, but they lost the phone connection."

My heart started pounding. *I will destroy anyone or anything in that house that hurts my babies.* I quickly picked up the office phone and called her back. "What's wrong, Tabitha? Did you phone?" I could hear my grandson laughing in the background.

"You need to come home, Mom," she said. "We need to talk."

"Okay, I was on my way out the door when the front desk clerk said you called and seemed upset. It sounds like the baby is happy."

"Oh, yes, he is delighted. I can't say the same for the dog or cat though. I will tell you when you get home. You're coming now, right?"

I arrived home and witnessed Muggsy guarding Tabitha and Nicky. He was on full alert, standing directly in front of them as they sat on the couch so no one could get near. He caught a glimpse of me coming around the corner and greeted me with a whimper of relief.

Tabitha had a look of disbelief on her face and said, "You have got to be kidding me."

Nicky was sitting on her lap. Her packed bags were on the floor and an empty glass of wine next to a large kitchen knife put on the side table to the left.

"Do I need to fill up that glass of wine for this conversation, Tabitha?"

"Yes," said Tabitha, "I am surprised you are not an alcoholic by now living in this house."

Tabitha said she was in the kitchen, getting supper started. The cat was sitting on the floor next to Nicky, who was lying down on the blanket. All of a sudden, the cat was hissing with his back up in a defensive position. He let out a scream and ran out of the house through the doggy door. "I ran into the living room to find Muggsy straddled over Nicky and growling into the air. I tried to calm him down, but he was letting me know something was there, and he was not going to let them get to Nicky. Then for no reason, he just sat down next to the blanket with his paw up like he was giving it to someone, and he was calm." Then Tabitha continued, with her voice shaking. "Someone hoisted Nicky up on to his feet and was holding and balancing him right there right in front of me. I think Nicky could see them. I think the dog and cat could as well. The cat wanted nothing to do with it. Muggsy, once feeling he needed to protect us, went to complete acceptance, and Nicky was happy and content."

I tried to get Tabitha to breathe and slow down, trying to make light of the situation. "Well, whoever it was, they liked you, the baby, and the dog, right?"

Tabitha said she did not think that was the point. She was used to strange things happening all around her growing up. It became everyday life, almost normal. As a teenager, she thought it was very cool to have a witch for a mother. It was not until she moved out and away from those incidences that it hit her that those kinds of occurrences were not the norm, and they could be harmful. It all came rushing back twofold with her presence in the house. Tabitha wanted to know if the spirits were always that active and robust. I said, "No, I believe it is because you are here. Tabitha, you understand, and I know you have the same sight as me. The difference is I have embraced it as much as I would allow, and you choose to close it out. You can keep the door closed. That is your choice, but it doesn't just make it go away. You have restricted their entry, but it is just a barrier because, at one time, you did request the knowledge and you did open up the door. As soon as you did that even once, your energy became visible, and you became sensitive to lower vibrating energy as well as higher vibrating energy, which was thrilled to experience you. It is not a bad thing, Tabitha. You have power over all of it. Nothing can hurt you unless you believe it can."

Tabitha said that she knew and was not ready or willing to live with them yet, especially now that there was a baby in the picture. She said she needed to figure out her options.

After having this experience, Tabitha decided the immediate action to take would be to work as a waitress/bartender, wherein cash would come fast, and make the best of it temporarily. Tabitha had decided she would find two or three other single parents and rent a house, and maybe one of them would play the stay-home mom/dad and watch the kids while the others went to work. She said she understood that I had to be there at the house, and she hoped I would be there alone for a while and finish learning what I needed to learn. Tabitha said, "I love you, and please come and visit us soon because we will not be back."

I tried not to talk to anyone about the house, especially the hotel and university staff, because I didn't want to be labeled a weirdo and not corporate enough for the management company that they took very seriously.

My manager, Susan, was vigilant and persistent, wanting to know what transpired with my daughter. Susan picked up on a few details about the house that intrigued her enough that she asked if she could come over and visit me after work one day. Susan would be my first visit that was not family since the police officer was there. I was thrilled and told her, "Yes, follow me home."

We entered through the front door as I did not want Muggsy to scare her if we went around to the back. Plus, it was a more delightful entrance.

Susan walked and immediately displayed a big grin. "How cute this place is, and I love that you are not afraid of using color. I have never seen someone use this shade of blue on their kitchen walls and evergreen for the living room, and what is that antique yellow in the dining room? I would never have the nerve, but you know it works and goes very well with your furniture. Did you paint the walls to match the furniture you already had?"

"Sure, we can go with that," I muttered to myself. I did not want to tell her the house came that way because it was waiting for me and my furniture to arrive. It was not me with the excellent artist's taste. Instead, I just said, "Thank you, I am glad you like it." I laughed and declared, "Okay, the

first-floor tour is completed. Would you like to see upstairs?" I led Susan to
the wooden stairway.

"I love these old staircases," she said. "They have such character." Susan
was a few steps behind me and suddenly stopped before she finished catching
up with me. She shivered, and all the hair was standing up straight on her
arms and head as if an electrical current was running through her entire body.

"Oh my god, what was that, Augusta?"

"I am so sorry. Did that hurt you and scare you, Susan?" I forgot that
besides Luke, my daughter, and the police officer, no one else has been in the
house since I moved in, and the officer never left the kitchen, and Luke had a
lot of adjusting to do. Once he settled in, these little happenings calmed down.

"Wow, I am fine, Augusta, I have been aware of particular and different
energy before in places, but I have never felt anything this strong before.
I'm fine. Don't worry—I think I'm just feeling a bit anxious. Let's just keep
going."

"Susan, the house likes you or at least likes your strength, which is a
good thing."

We reached the second bedroom, and we both experienced icy-cold
temperatures. We could see our breath, and we exited as fast as we could.

"I don't like that room, Augusta. What is going on in there?"

"It is a long story, but if you want to know, I will try to explain it to you
some other time."

We proceeded downstairs, and Susan gave me a big hug. "I have to
provide you with credit living here and staying alone. I had to see this house
for myself, and now I have firsthand knowledge that the rumors are true. I
would keep this to yourself though unless you want all the nuts and religiously
righteous people camping out on your front lawn. Please keep what is going
on here quiet, especially at work, but of course, you can tell me everything.
I'm intrigued and would like updates. Be careful, Augusta, I also feel this
house could consume you."

Although intrigued, I knew Susan, and she would not be back. She was
too focused on her fast-track career and desires and would not be distracted
by anyone or anything.

I found a local carpenter to work on the barn. I noticed every morning
that before he entered to start work, he would make the sign of the cross,
breathe deeply with his eyes shut, and muster all his inner strength before
beginning. I invited him several times to come into the house and rest during

his break time, but he never took me up on my offer. He never asked any questions and did not want me to give him any answers. He was there to do a job and get out. I felt a little bad as I know he thought he accepted the position from hell. He was from the old school: a verbal commitment and a handshake was a contract, and he was there to finish the job. He also did not want to come across as a weak man who allowed fear to rule him. I was impressed with that, and I knew I had chosen the right guy for the job.

The barn was ready for my Sonny to come to live here and for Luke for his second visit. It was vital for me to get ready for this visit. I needed to understand why some people had closed minds when it came to other possibilities and felt threatened in a house like this while other minds were open and not threatened.

Chapter 15

Open and Closed Minds

I loved communicating with Jonathan, and learning about closed and open minds was one of my favorite lessons. Jonathan asked, "Do you know you are just using part of your brain?"

"Yeah, what the heck is wrong with the rest of it? Is the rest of my brain empty?"

Jonathan answered, "Every person is capable of receiving and experiencing all levels of frequency, but most of us do not allow this to happen. Only lower vibrations, which are the most restricted, are permitted. They are the ones that give us acceptance with the rest of the world. We push away thoughts and imagination if it doesn't fit into the limited thinking of our society and our family, the church, or the government. When we do this, we close off all other possibilities if they don't have a place within our perceived value system.

"Do you remember your parents telling you if you wanted it bad enough, you could have it and your Sunday Bible study teacher preaching to you that anything was possible and you just have to believe and have faith? Then as soon as you started to imagine things that were different from what they thought and felt, they pulled you back and told you to come back down to reality. They said you were a daydreamer, and you had to conform to be accepted and survive in this world, so incomplete contradiction, the limitation of your creativity, begins. Now you are becoming closed-minded. Being closed-minded means you reject the possibilities of a more-excellent reality, the options of afterlife, and the chance that even evil is not evil—it is something else. Every time you allow and accept a thought that is different from the norm to enter your brain, it starts a chain reaction: your pituitary gland opens up more and more each time you are willing to receive another thought. People use meditation techniques to help open up their pituitary glands. We're so awed by people who we think are geniuses, but all they've done is open up the possibilities of 'what if?' All you've got to do is know yourself, quiet your mind, and listen. Recognize the potential when it presents itself."

"Is it my job or destiny to teach this knowingness to everyone? Is that why I am here? Is that why I know things and always feel I have to move forward toward something? What am I supposed to do with this?"

"Augusta, it is not your job to teach anyone this unless they seek you out. The only responsibility you have is to yourself. You are here, and you have this knowledge because you asked to know. After all, even as a young child, you opened your mind to other possibilities. You opened the floodgates. You've retained the memories of out-of-body encounters as a child and as an adult. You've visited some of these other planes in both life and death. This place is here to teach you—not for you to teach others. You will be ready to leave this house when you have found what it is you need to understand. This place has drawn people here for thousands of years. This place, like many others on your earth, radiates an energy field that attracts other types of energy. Some answer the call. Some do not."

"What am I going to do when it comes to my husband? He just thinks there are evil ghosts in the house, and that they have to go."

"Don't be as hard on him as you still have a certain level of doubt yourself about what resides here. He calls them ghosts, and you call them entities. He thinks there needs to be an exorcism, and you think they just need help to move on—the same outcome, just different methods. The problem is you will never purify this house completely because as many as you have already woken up and assisted on to another level, many will take their place. You will not change the way it has been for thousands of years. When you have moved on, another will take your place."

Chapter 16

My First Winter Back

I was about to experience my first winter season for many years in the northeast. I had forgotten how cold it could get. Christmas and New Year's had come and gone, and now that the airfares were a reasonable price again, Luke was on his way back for his third visit. The Florida house was on the market; no keen buyers yet, but I knew it would sell when the time was right.

Luke and I caught up with all of our life news. Luke was only able to stay for ten days this time as he had a big job to start on his return to Florida and he wanted to be there for any potential home buyers. His goal this visit was to (with help from some family members) build me that paddock area for my horse's arrival in March.

I went off to work that day, and Luke was thrilled to be able to enter the barn from the fifteen-foot-high sliding door that was fixed by the carpenter the week before. We purchased hardware and a small stable stepladder to hang saddles, bridles, and ropes. Luke sensed a presence with him, and the goosebumps appeared on his arms. He brushed it off as a chill in the air and his paranoia, moving on to the first level of the ladder. Instinctively, Luke realized that something was wrong. There was someone else in the barn with him, and with that single thought, the stepladder pushed out underneath him, and the last thing he recalled was his head hitting the sawdust floor.

Susan entered my office, motioning me to end my call, which I did immediately. "Augusta, we received a phone call from one of your neighbors that said your husband had some kind of accident. The police are there trying to calm down your huge dog so they can get close enough to help him. Go home immediately. They know you are on your way and will be there in five minutes."

I held my breath all the way, driving down Stone Road and viewed two police cars and an ambulance. Thank God Luke was sitting up in the driveway with Muggsy still standing over him in full protective mode. I jumped out of the truck and reassured Muggsy that it was okay to let the friendly people help his master.

"What happened?" I asked as the paramedics placed Luke on a stretcher.

My neighbor Mary, an older woman in her late seventies, stepped up with a quick explanation of what she saw, which was not much. "I saw your dog pulling your husband out of the barn by his shirt collar to the driveway. I was not sure if he was helping him or attacking him. Then Muggsy started to wail and bark to get someone's attention. I called the police, and they were here in minutes, but your dog was not going to let anyone near him. I knew you were close, so I asked them not to hurt the dog, that you could handle him."

I followed the ambulance to the hospital emergency entrance. The attendant asked me to stay in the waiting room, and they would let me know when I could come in and see Luke. I knew he was going to be okay as he was talking and telling me he was all right and not to worry.

The doctors were shocked: not only did he have a fractured foot, but his foot and heel were smashed and held together by his battered, swollen skin keeping his toes in place. "Augusta, that kind of damage is usually seen either when someone falls from a very high point right on their feet or when something substantial has been thrown down on top of them. According to your husband, he was just twelve inches off the ground, and there was nothing in the barn that could cause this injury. We will transport him to the trauma center in Putnam where a surgeon will be there to repair his foot as best he can."

My heart sunk to know that this wasn't just a freak accident. Is this a futile effort on the part of one of the not-so-beautiful people in the house to let him know he wasn't accepted there? It was going to be a long rehab, and Luke was going to be homebound for at least six to eight weeks. That was a kick in the butt to the asshole who hurt him. They wanted him out, and now he was staying even longer.

I was able to take three days off to be with Luke during his crucial recovery time. He was looking at me now with hate in his eyes that was replaced by a pure panic that I would even think about leaving him there alone with them to go back to work. He was on a lot of medication, drifting in and out of sleep, muttering, "They will not be happy until they kill me."

I knew I could not leave him alone. I called my mother and sister Jane to see if they could come and stay with us for about a week to help him through this difficult time. They reluctantly agreed as the family had to be there for each other, but they said they were bringing their Bibles, and their prayer group would be coming at some point to bless the house.

I had a hospital bed set up in the living room, which was okay with Luke as the last place he wanted to be was stuck up in that bedroom. He was not staying there even if he could make it up the stairs, which was impossible for him.

Mom and Jane arrived the night before I had to return to work the next day. The only place I could give them to sleep was the second bedroom. It had two twin beds and one dresser for their clothes. They did not mention the coldness of the room, but it was January in an old house, and the room had a chill to it.

I pleaded with the house and my protector Jonathan to watch over them. "Please, I need them to stay to help me. Don't let anything weird happen."

Neither one said they felt anything terrible in the house; if they did, they made sure not to let on for Luke's sake.

We stayed up that evening pretty late, keeping Luke preoccupied, waiting for him to fall asleep before we headed up to bed. Mom and Jane settled in and were thankful I had extra blankets for their chilly bedroom. I heard Jane say to Mom through the walls, "Wow, I can see my breath, but I don't feel any drafts."

As I lay in my bed, I tried to contact Jonathan, but he chose to be silent. I guess he was giving me space while my family was visiting. I was happy that the rest of the house was also quiet—for a while anyway.

I was woken from a deep sleep by a loud bang and talking coming from the hallway toward my closed door.

"Augusta, Augusta, we are coming in." The door opened simultaneously.

Mom and Jane, with looks of terror on their faces, said, "We are not sleeping in that room, so either we all sleep in your bed or we set up downstairs and sleep there."

Luke woke up with all the commotion and yelled to us, "What is going on up there!"

"Sorry, Luke, we are coming down."

It was three in the morning, giving us only four hours of sleep, and I had to work in the morning.

We all huddled down on the couch in the living room, and I said I would make everyone warm herbal tea, and they could tell me what the problem was. I know it was wishful thinking that the house, especially that room, would behave itself through the night.

Mom started her story first, "I was awakened a little by what I thought was Jane getting up to use the toilet. I was sleeping peacefully before that, mind you. I did not give it much thought and fell back to sleep only to be awakened again with someone spooning me. I felt their body right up against mine and their arms around me. I thought that Jane got confused coming back from the bathroom and ended up hugging me in my bed, thinking that she was hugging Billy, her husband. I said, 'Jane, you are in the wrong bed' and then heard Jane say from across the room, 'What? What do you mean? No, I'm not.' I jolted up to a sitting position, and Jane sprang to her feet as I felt and she saw my bed bounce back into place as the door was flung open and then shut again on its own. Oh my god, Augusta, I have not slept with anybody since your father died, and I have no intention of starting now!"

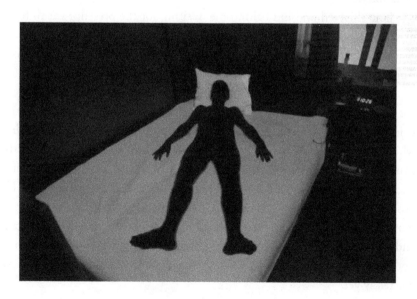

Luke sat up in bed and smiled. He was vindicated. "See, you guys. I know down deep you thought I was crazy, but I am not mad. There is something not right about this house. I am right, right?"

Jane looked at me and then at Luke and said, "I didn't want to say anything before, but I knew it as soon as I walked into the house."

I kept quiet, waiting for the bomb to drop, telling me they could not stay. My mother turned to me and stated, "Augusta, I know you are not religious and do not believe in the Church, but if you want us to stay, you have to agree to allow me to call in my prayer group and Pastor Steve to clean this house."

Jane chimed in with, "Yes definitely."

And Luke said, "I don't care if it will help."

I was out-voiced three to one, so I conceded.

It was time to get ready to go to work. With no sleep, it was not going to be a good day. Jane stood at the kitchen sink, cleaning the early-morning teacups as Mom and I entered from around the corner. Jane froze in place; her eyes were as wide as one could make them, and her hair was floating right behind her as if someone were playing with her. "What's going on here, guys?"

She could feel it, and we could see it, and seeing it transpire while others were present placed the otherwise-familiar occurrences on a whole new level for me. I muttered to myself, "Damn it, you just could not behave, could you, house?!"

Jane shivered and hid behind me, waiting for the presence we all felt to dissipate. Jane said, looking toward Mom, "Is it too early to call Pastor Steve?"

Luke, leaning on his crutches and smirking, said sarcastically, "Good one, Augusta, you have made your dreams a nightmare for everyone else."

I went off to work, and I knew as soon as the hour was respectable, they would be rallying the troops to come to the house. I did not want to be there while they prayed at my home. I had my doubts about the outcome of this ritual and did not want to be a part of it. They may be able to help the positive energies move on, but they were just going to piss off the negative ones. The positive energy, or good ghosts, were looking and willing to accept help to move on. The others who were dubbed the Antichrist, the devil, or wicked and evil were just misunderstood, frightened, and lost ghosts. They would not recognize the light the priest and prayer group offer because they were not ready yet.

I was able to leave early from work that day because Susan had asked me to come in for a few hours that weekend. When I arrived home, it was around 4:00 PM, and the sun had just started to go down. *Shit, they are still there standing in the side yard. I guess they are blessing the barn also.*

Father Steve said, "I believe we have helped, and the house is clean for now, but it would not hurt for you, Augusta, to pray and find God also to keep them away. We will pray for you too."

I must have heard the word *believe* and *faith* twenty times within ten minutes. I wanted to scream at them all about how I felt about their belief and faith and what it meant to me. I said nothing as there was no reason to attack or hurt them because these were the beliefs that made them happy; this was their reality, and I had no right to inflict my thoughts on them. My thoughts were my reality, and not theirs.

To me, as soon as someone chooses to believe in something or chooses to have blind faith, it means they have not yet reached "knowing." Either one knows knowingness or they don't. If you have faith, you can only believe, but you don't really know, and if you have to rely on faith, you only think (the belief) that someday you might know. It is very confusing saying this even to myself. There are no words to explain it any better.

Jane and Mom made it through the rest of the week, and I was very grateful for their help and for watching over Luke so I could concentrate on work and not worry about him. They could leave now as he was going to get around on crutches. He was able to make his way back to the kitchen and the bathroom. They were more than ready to get on their way, and I knew they weren't going to be back. No one had ever come back.

We received a phone call from Jill, the one friend who always kept in touch with me throughout the years. It did not matter if either of us had vivid memories of our past together; we just always felt a connection even if we had spent years apart. Jill, her husband, Marvin, and their daughter, Lilly, were in Connecticut for a visit and wanted to stop by for a one-night stay. I was thrilled and felt it was good for Luke to have friends visit.

They arrived midafternoon; Luke was still struggling to get around on his crutches but managed to let them enter through the front door. Poor Marvin was not but five steps into the front hall when he tripped or was tripped, smashing into the wall. He had no idea what happened and was a little embarrassed. When we suggested we all go out for an early supper, they jumped at the idea and wanted to hear all about the house on neutral ground. We tried to keep the conversation light so as not to scare Lilly, but she said she already had a feeling the house was haunted, and we did not have to sugarcoat it for her.

After dinner, we went back to the house, and we talked for many hours. We had set up the upstairs back bedroom for them. Marvin and Jill would share one bed, and Lilly would sleep in the other. They were fighting sleep, but the day of traveling made them very tired they gave in.

Luke and I heard them talking in the middle of the night though we could not make out what they were saying. It sounded like Jill was trying to console Lilly.

We all met in the kitchen for breakfast the next morning. Lilly started to tell us about the man she saw at the end of her bed that night, and Marvin and Jill were trying to assure her that their active imaginations were due to the stories they had been told that night. Nevertheless their bags were packed, and they were more than ready to leave. They gave the excuse that a snowstorm was predicted, and they needed to beat the storm. I did not expect to see them again as long as I was living in the house.

The February storm came in fast, and the snow fell, blanketing the field; ice formed over the water, and one could hear a strange singing coming from the distance. My neighbors told me the music I heard was that of the ice melting and the water flowing under the ice. Everything was lovely.

My horse was coming soon, sometime in March, and Luke had plans all ready to return to Florida. I went back to the barn to admire the work done on the horse paddock and see if anything needed to be purchased other than hay and feed. The snow crunched under my boots, cracking the thin layer of ice that had formed from the day's melting and the night's freezing. I was sure to be careful holding on to the railing that descended to the back of the barn so I would not slip. I shimmied in between the fence rails into the paddock area. I immediately slid down on my butt from the top of the enclosure to the opposite end. I braced myself for the accident that I was about to suffer. The entire area was an ice rink, with just the right incline to be a death trap for my horse and for me to break a leg. The constant melting and freezing had caused significant dips in the ground throughout the enclosure, and top level, the area would cost not only a lot of working hours but also a lot of money. There was no way Sonny could come home. Even if all the snow and ice melted, the incline would erode every time it rained. My heart sank, and I became despondent as I went back inside.

Luke knew by the stressed look on my face, something was wrong. "Oh no, now what, Augusta?

"We can't bring Sonny here in March because it is not safe for him in the paddock. The whole area is full of ice and ruts. He will break his leg!"

"Augusta, the ice will melt, so it will be fine. It is going to warm up this afternoon, and all the ice will be gone. Don't worry."

"It is not just the ice, Luke. It is all the holes and ruts. The entire enclosure needs leveling. It would take truckloads of dirt and many working hours to fix. We don't have the time or the money right now. Next month, I was looking forward to seeing Sonny. I might have to wait until the end of the spring or the summer to see him again."

"I am so sorry, Augusta. Something will work out. It always does for you."

I did not sleep well that night. I kept thinking about the barn situation, and Luke was restless also. I heard a lot of noise I thought was coming from downstairs but did not want to investigate. I just wanted to hide under my covers and feel sorry for myself. I must have dozed off in the wee morning hours and was not up bright and early on Sunday morning as I usually was. I probably would have continued sleeping if Luke was not calling for me from the bottom of the stairs. "Augusta, are you awake? You need to wake up and see this."

I stumbled out of bed wrapped up in my fuzzy bathrobe, slipped on some socks, and proceeded down the stairs only to see Luke fully dressed and leaning on his crutches with one boot on as well as a hat, gloves, and winter coat.

"What are you doing, Luke? Are you crazy going outside by yourself? What is so crucial that you could not wait for me?"

"You will see, Augusta. Put your coat on and look! I can't believe this, and I just don't know what to say. It is amazing!"

I helped Luke down the back steps. Thankfully, the temperatures had warmed up, and there was no more ice, only a little mud. Luke stood on the top of the stairs, heading to the back of the barn, and he asked me to go down and look.

I didn't have to go too far to see what it was all about. "What the hell! I don't understand what happened. Do I see this correctly?"

The ice was gone as well as the holes and ruts. The area was flat and level and was fit to be a riding ring as well as a paddock enclosure. The tears started to roll down my face, and I ran up, hugging Luke. "Do you see this, Luke? Is it not something? Oh my god, it is so beautiful."

"Yes, Augusta, it is something or something else. It is obvious the house wants you to be happy. You were sad, so something fixed it for you. Don't get me wrong, Augusta—I am thrilled, but this is not right. These things don't happen to ordinary people. I guess I don't have to worry about you when I am gone. God help the person who tries to hurt you here."

Luke left, I wanted him to stay longer, but he had to join me on his terms and his own time. I felt terrible he had to recuperate the rest of the way by himself, but he insisted it was time for him to return to Florida. Either he'd come for another visit in three or four months if the house in Florida still hadn't sold or he'd come to stay for good if it did.

I knew it would be longer than a few months for Luke to return, even for a visit. He was angry with me, and felt I was choosing the house over him, and in a way, he was right.

Chapter 17

Questions and Answers

I took this extended opportunity of alone time to learn more from Jonathan. "Jonathan, can we discuss my purpose again, my destiny, God's plan?"

"Augusta, there is no plan. If God had a set plan or predetermined destiny for you, that would be taking your freedom away, your ability to express and grow in knowledge. That is why you are here on earth to learn to experience, to manifest, to wake up. There is only the now, be in the 'is-ness' of things. You always have the option to change at any moment you want. Your purpose in life is to be a part of it. You and you alone are the creators. You can become whatever you desire if you allow yourself. That is everyone's destiny—unlimited freedom."

"Jonathan, what about following God's laws and the Church's laws? If we follow those laws, doesn't that automatically curb unlimited freedom?

"Augusta, yes, indeed, it does. God has made no laws. Humans have made laws. Humans added the phrase 'it is the law of God.' It gives the human-made law power and credence because people have learned to surrender themselves to God and fear him if they don't obey 'the law of God.' Man is the law creator, not God."

"Jonathan, what if there were no laws? Everybody would be running around doing anything they wanted and any evil thing they wanted, hurting people along the way. How would we stop them?"

"Augusta, let me first tell you that there is no such thing as evil, just as there is no such thing as something being good. I know this is a difficult concept for you to swallow, but listen to me. Let's go with the Bible, the written book of God, 'God's laws.' This is the easiest way to begin, but remember that humans have written the Bible, and humans have limited knowledge. Everything is part of God, and God is everything. If that statement is right and evil is in the world, that would mean that God has darkness within him, and he doesn't. God just is. The soul just is, it is not holding evil or good. It holds experiences and expresses those experiences with actions and thought. Humans are the ones who look around and judge what is right and what is evil. God cannot look down and judge himself. Humans are the creator of good and evil, and some very enlightened people wrote laws and rules into books to help humankind understand and learn. The most important lesson they have to teach is 'Do unto others as you would have them do unto you.'"

"Why is this so important?"

"Because if you wanted to term anything evil, it would be when someone tries to or succeeds in taking someone else's freedom or denies them life and the right to their experiences. Anything you do to another that stops them, limits them, or puts judgment on them becomes part of your truth, your reality, your consciousness. By doing that, you have defined and limited yourself with that action, and you have judged yourself, which puts you further and further away from knowing God. Look at life as a maze. You wander around looking for the center, which is the goal for everyone who enters the labyrinth. You make mistakes. You take wrong turns. You learn from your mistakes. Sometimes, you end up right at the beginning. When entities enter the maze, they are not sure what is in the center. They have only been told and instructed that it is their ultimate and most important goal, and if they can reach the center, they find God and live forever."

"Jonathan, what about murder? Jonathan, are you telling me that killing isn't evil?"

"Augusta, I don't want to answer that question as you are not yet able to comprehend the answer, but you asked, so yes and no. It is evil because the murder cut short their victims' chance for the experience. It is evil because mankind is instinctively destructive and needs to learn to curb his appetite. Evil is a word and a state of mind that humankind has created. Who's going to say that dying is wrong? Humans? Remember, everyone has a choice when and how they return to learn from an experience to gain knowledge and knowingness. Maybe the person who has been raped, tortured, or murdered asked to experience that lesson because they were at one time the person committing the murder and they are trying to make their way through the maze. The murderer might have once been the person who was abused and needs to feel the experience of revenge. You should not feel bad for who you think the victim is in this scenario because I told you there is nothing called death. You live forever—just in a different consciousness. If you're going to feel sorry for someone, it should be for the murderer because they have a long way to go and a lot of practice before they can break through and figure out the circle, finding their way out of the labyrinth."

Short Explanation

My head was spinning with this altered possibility. Jonathan was right; I was not ready to comprehend that answer. I wouldn't let go of the response I got because I had asked the question; I did have the thought, and I wanted to know. I tried to understand all the options for things being the way they were, an explanation for all the chaos I felt and saw. It was so hard to know and to let go of things I was taught to believe. I had been programmed. Did I honestly know? It made even more sense to me why I agreed to give up my childhood memories and only keep the ones that were the most important for me to experience—what I ask for without carrying all the extra baggage. I emptied my mind of all the nonessential thoughts so I could learn easier.

Possibilities

1. Is this the truth? Yes, as there are many truths and multiple possibilities.
2. Are ghosts real? Yes, depending on your interpretation, a ghost can be harmful or positive energy, spirits, or entities looking for a way to move on. Some are more confused than others. Some are so confused that they don't realize they have physically died.
3. Is there good and evil? Yes and no. Yes, as humankind has produced the words and placed judgment on actions as being right or wrong to keep order and control chaos in the world they live in. No, because God is everything, and God is good; God is not evil, so nothing is inherently evil. Good and evil are manifested through humankind's experiences.
4. Is there life after death? Seeing that there is no such thing as death, then no, but yes to the afterlife.

5. Are there such things as angels? Yes, but humankind is more advanced than angels. Humankind is closer to God than angels are. They are simply energy and have not yet experienced humans. They can't have compassion, sympathy, or understand you because they have never been you. They will eventually become God/humanlike but not yet, so they are still angels.

6. Is there reincarnation and karma? Yes, but it is entirely up to you if you want to return to earth. Humankind allows the body to die; you are only giving up your body but not your life. Life is endless. Karma is coming back to learn what you did not learn the last time you were here on this plane. Karma is not someone else getting revenge.

7. Is there a god? Of course, there is a god. You have been taught that Jesus is the Son of God—a humanoid vibrating on a much higher energy level than his brothers here on this earth. So you can say that Jesus has God's essence as a part of him, and because of that, he was able to perform miracles such as ascending into the heavens after his human body was released. Some are taught that he will come back to us one day but currently does not choose to. Just as we can return through reincarnation if we decide to time and time again. We have also been told by Jesus that we are all his brothers. That would mean we also hold somewhere deep inside us, the same essence, or for lack of a better name, DNA. That means we, too, can perform miracles; we have just forgotten that we are divine. Technically humankind is God. Our journey, our ultimate goal, is to find our way home to God to ourselves.

8. What is the purpose of life? Life is a journey of experiences and choices that brings knowledge. One's purpose in life is to live it.

Chapter 18

Living Alone

I was getting very comfortable being single. I was married, but not in the traditional sense. Luke wasn't trying to visit me any longer. I thought he might be trying to break away from me and find someone else back in Florida to keep him company. I wasn't mad, which scared me; indifference usually meant the death of a relationship. I realized I had no right to be mad at him. He might have another experience waiting for him. The life with me and the knowledge he needed to learn, know, and feel might have come full circle, and it was now time for him to move on. I had to accept this reality if I was going to continue my journey through the maze.

I had a good job and was bringing home a decent paycheck. Luke needed to keep more of his earnings in Florida for his expenses, and I thought it would be good to rent out the second bedroom to a male coworker who unexpectedly found he needed temporary living accommodations. It would be nice to have a little extra money coming in as well as a male presence.

Rick was about five years younger than me, a single father with visiting rights to see his seven-year-old son every other weekend. He had only a duffle bag of clothes and some personal items, which was perfect because a woman would have had so much more and there were no closets or storage in the house for accommodating another woman.

When showing him the room, I apologized for the sparseness and the chill in the air, but he was okay with it and said he would just put on the little space heater I had in case there was a cold night. "I don't have much as you can see, so I don't need much."

At the end of week one, I asked Rick how he was doing in his room. He looked tired and a little drawn. He said he was doing fine but was having a lot of weird dreams that woke him up a couple of times a night. I asked if he remembered what he dreamed about. He said it was always the same recurring dream about a little girl with a pink ribbon in her hair. Sometimes she was just playing on the floor or trying to get me to go up into the attic, and then other times, she was crying, holding her stomach as if it hurt, and she was very sick.

At the end of week two, Rick started to miss days at work from an illness he said he must have picked up—a stomach virus. During this time, he would not leave his bedroom unless he needed to get liquids or make some soup. It got worse as the weeks went by. He missed more work and started to show deep dark circles under his eyes, and he was exhausted and would have to drag himself down the stairs into the kitchen.

I would come home from work some days and know he had not moved or had anything to eat or drink. I would bring him tea and food when possible, only to find it the next day untouched. I asked him to go to the doctor to call a friend or family member to help him, but he refused. He was going to die up in that room unless I did something fast. He was not thinking clearly and was complaining he had pain in his stomach, but it would come and go. I took action and found his brother who lived about an hour away. It was evident they were not close, and he was more annoyed that I called for his assistance than concerned for Rick's well-being.

Nevertheless, he came and took Rick to the area hospital. I followed up once Rick was out of danger and able to speak to me by phone. He said his intestines developed large blisters, and he was going into septic shock from the infection. They called it inflamed Crohn's disease. They found it very unusual; usually, a person would have previous symptoms of this disease, and in his case, it just came on all of a sudden. He would have died in a matter of days if he had not been admitted into the hospital when he was.

Rick thanked me for calling his brother and getting him help and was sorry he did not listen to me sooner. He'd be hospitalized for another week then stop by and get his things from the house. He would be staying with his brother until he completely healed. I guess whatever went wrong between them at one time was figured out.

Two years of living in the house were approaching. I spoke to Luke now about three times a week and not every day as we used to. I developed new relationships and immersed myself in my job. One day I just decided it was time to take a stand on where our relationship was going. I told him I loved him and wanted him to come, and I knew there was an offer on the house, and he should accept it. If he was going to work out the financial details and figure out how he could stay in Florida with me in Connecticut and file for divorce, we should do that, but we had to make a decision.

He did take a few days to contemplate what I said. I think it was hard for him to accept that I showed no anger in my statement. I told him what I wanted, but it was ultimately his choice, and he had to make one as I was moving forward.

Luke joined me after the Florida house closing. He was walking without assistance, but the healing process took a very long time both physically and emotionally. Upon joining me, Luke came back with the belief that everything that had happened before in the house could be explained away with logic and bad luck. It was the only way he could deal with it; he had to take his power back. I was okay with that and understood him to be like most other people who had experienced the house; after departing, they reasoned their experiences away or felt as long as they did not come back to the house, they would not have to deal with it. The churchgoers brought them closer to God. The believers of ghosts immersed themselves in a supernatural occult, and others just closed their minds to it and refused to ever think of it again. I understood this was not their experience. They did not ask to know; this was for me and me alone.

Not Living Alone

It was only about one week after Luke's move-in date, and I started to feel an overwhelming anger building inside of me. I was depressed, uneasy, unsettled, and anxious. I had little or no time now to meditate and speak with Jonathan. I felt disconnected from the house as Luke was taking more of my time and attention. Sometimes when I looked in the mirror, I did not recognize myself. What I saw was nothing—a face with no features. I had no eyes. I could no longer see.

I would go with my horse for all-day rides on the weekend to the local parks or sometimes for hours in the field behind the house. It was something I could do alone and think as we had only one horse at the time, and it was reasonable to say I had to exercise him.

Luke was anxious as he needed to find employment and could no longer do manual labor daily with his newly healed foot, and he was also angry to know his life would never be the same. Luke hated change, and I tried so hard to be sympathetic and wanted to make our marriage work. He spent his first week building me a pasture fence as he was so good that, and he knew that Sonny needed to graze. I would occasionally help, but he wanted this to be his project and only requested my assistance from time to time. The paddock area stayed perfect—no ruts, no holes, not even any mud. Luke never brought up the weirdness of this phenomenon again because, though he had no idea how he convinced himself, there was a logical explanation.

All logic started to fly out the window after the second week of his return. Things began to go sideways. It was a little mischieflike stuff at first, and it made me snicker that he was being teased and mocked. Small things were happening, such as a hammer being moved some place other than where he had placed it or a plate sliding around the table. I felt it served him right as he utterly denied the life of the house, and they were gentle with little wake-up gestures thrown at him. They were trying to make it work with him, but he was ignoring them, so more specific things began to happen.

Sitting on the couch one evening as I was cleaning in the kitchen, Luke saw the curtains by the front door moving, and he felt a chill and cold breeze enter the living room. He asked me if I had left a window open by any chance upstairs as there was a draft. I told him I did not think so, but stranger things had happened, so there could be. He got up from the couch and headed for the stairs, and from the corner of my eye, I saw him jump back about five feet from the stairs, and he let out a "What the fuck?"

I quickly ran over to him and asked what was wrong. He said, "Swear to God, Augusta, a little girl was standing on the top of the stairs dressed in old vintage clothing. She had blonde hair and was holding a little doll, I think."

Wow! I had not seen anyone materialize in the house before, except Jonathan, and I wondered why this young girl showed herself to Luke. I told him I was sorry I missed it. Luke wanted to know if I believed him, and I said, "Of course I do, and I also know that all the other little things happening to you are not your imagination either."

"Why didn't you say anything? You just let me stumble around this house."

I told him it was because he came back refusing to acknowledge the life in the house, so I gave up and was not going to push the issue. Plus, they were not being mean; they were just playing with him.

He said to me, "But, Augusta, I see the change in you, and it is not a good one. You might not notice it, but I do, and you are not looking well either.

You walk around this house like a zombie and are angry all the time like you are possessed. I didn't want to let you know, Augusta, but I have done some investigation on my own, and I can get some people that have worked with cleaning houses of spirits and ghosts. I told them just some of the issues, and they are willing to come out next week and take a look. Depending on what they find, they might need to stay here for a few days. I love the house, and I want to stay here with you, but you have to be willing to work with me."

I tried to discourage Luke from taking this route and reminded him that the priest and prayer group did not affect the house, so what did he think these ghost hunters were going to do? Luke said he did not know, but they had all kinds of equipment as well as sensitive and clairvoyant people, not just a Bible and holy water. I agreed because I was feeling off as well, and the positive energy was losing ground to the negative in the house; my feel-good mood was gone, and I was unable to contact Jonathan.

Chapter 19

Ghost Busters

It was 6:00 PM and dark when the first crew arrived. They stood outside with flashlights awhile, taking pictures and walking the property before they came knocking at the front door to introduce themselves. There were four of them. They did not want to talk right away. They wanted to immediately walk through the house alone from the attic down to the basement and said we would all sit down and talk when they finished. They spent approximately forty-five minutes with the lights off and flashlights on, taking notes, pictures, and audio and video.

Once they had completed their self-tour, they came and joined us in the living room, and the first person to talk was the clairvoyant, Kelly. "This house has some ancient energy. These energies have been here way before the house. It's not the home. It's the land on which the house sits. Augusta, you are very sensitive to this, and, Luke, you are caught up in it. I can't tell you much yet as I need to experience the home more."

The technician, James, spoke next. "While walking through the house, I did pick up on some unusual sounds. When I get back to my office, I will try to clean what I have recorded. To understand more, I will need to set up equipment in the most active areas of the home for twenty-four hours at least."

One of the young women was deep in thought. Karen was a sensitive spiritual guide; this is the name given in her circle. In the church world, some priests had this gift of guidance. She spoke after she turned and smiled at me and said, "Yeah, we will come back."

The last person to contribute to the consultation was the physicist, Gordon. He studied physics and energetics. He was there to scientifically explain any phenomena in the home by logical means and not spiritual ones. He said, "My meters are picking up a lot of electrical currents in the house, so yes, to understand why, we should come back."

The group felt it was worth coming back; apparently, they found ample justification. Ultimately, it was Luke's and my decision. Luke immediately said yes, but I was a little reluctant to agree so quickly. I asked the group who were looking at me for approval, "Depending on what you find in the house, can the activity increase or become benevolent because you are calling them out?"

The clairvoyant, Kelly, spoke up, "Augusta, that's always a possibility, and that's why you have to know whether you can deal with what's going on or whether you want us to see if we can help."

I shook my head in defeat and said, "I am okay with what is here, but I know Luke is not, so yes, come back under one condition."

"Of course, we are here to help you, so it will be under your terms."

"I know you do not ask for money from the people you support, but you do have a TV show and books and a large following, and that is how you make this a business. Whatever you use, such as recordings, information, and findings, you cannot use our names nor have any pictures that would divulge the location of this house or who we are."

"Fair enough, Augusta, we have a deal, and that provision can be applied."

Luke was thrilled and relaxed as he felt hope that on their return, either the house would finally become quiet or the scientist would give the logical nonghostly explanation and reason it all away.

They would return the following Friday night and stay through the weekend because they said it was important that both Luke and I were home while their investigation was active.

Friday came, and this time, they came with an unmarked van filled with equipment and a Native American woman called Mora. They brought her along because Karen said she felt that presence along with many others. It took the group a few hours to set up all the different technical equipment throughout the house and spent time in each room, asking me to join them but instructing Luke to stay in the living room. They said they would take shifts when sleep was needed, but someone would always be awake to monitor things. We were to assist them when asked, but otherwise, we should go about life as usual.

The first room they focused on was the second bedroom. I was not surprised because even if you were not sensitive, you could feel something sad and oppressive in that room. Sitting down on the bed, Karen asked if anyone wanted to talk to her. Karen, being sensitive, went almost immediately into a trance, breathing deeply, and you could see the hair on her arms stand up straight. In a trancelike state, she said, "Yes, Sarah, I can sense you. I am sorry your stomach hurts. How can we help you? Sarah, don't leave. Are you afraid of something? Don't go."

James set up with his equipment in the kitchen and asked what was happening in the room. He said the energy level spiked, and the temperature was fifteen degrees cooler than the rest of the house. We all went down to talk to him in the kitchen. Gordon had gone down to the basement, the one place I refused to go. He called up to us in the kitchen, "Hey, guys, are you getting this? I have a lot of electrical activity down here. I am going to look around for some exposed wires and maybe a moisture source. Many of my instruments have stopped working. The batteries appear depleted. Monitor what you can from up there."

Mora was walking around outside, very intent on what she was experiencing, and Kelly went to check on Luke in the living room. She asked Luke how he was doing, and he said with disappointment in his voice, "As well as one could imagine as I am left alone as usual in this house."

The group decided to keep the equipment running automatically in the kitchen and for us as a group to go from room to room together, not to split up. The only people who would be alone would be Mora and Luke. Mora continued her exploration outside and in the barn. Luke sat pouting on the couch. The rest of us headed to the attic and would work our way down. They had a recorder and microphone in hand, and Kelly had a piece of paper and pen to record observations. Luke wanted to know why he had to stay behind; he felt left out. They told him it was evident the energy in the house was directed negatively toward him, and it might be better that he was not in harm's way while they were trying to call them forward.

Karen turned toward me and asked if I had found anything in the house when we moved in that was unusual. I thought for a bit as we climbed up the narrow stairwell to the attic and remembered the items found under the floorboards. I had forgotten about them up until that point. Kelly asked if there was a pink ribbon and a small handmade doll among the items.

I said, "Yes, there was. I left them in the corner of the loft. I did not want to take them because they seemed to belong to the house. How did you know that?"

The loft was a place I did not mind being. It was bright and comfortable even though it had all the characteristics of an old dusty attic. I pointed out where the items were placed in the corner; Kelly picked them up, studying them. I asked Kelly again, "How did you know about the ribbon and the doll?"

She laughed, making light of the knowledge and said that is why she got the big bucks.

Karen now had the items in hand while the attic stayed quiet, and we all felt we could move back down the stairs to the second bedroom that was the passageway through to the attic. We all knew that room was active. Riley requested that we turn the lights off so that he could monitor any outside light coming into the bedroom or any entry point for drafts. He would check his monitors that were on autopilot downstairs later. They asked me if there was any noted activity in the bathroom or bedroom or the closet/computer room, and I said other than Luke saying it always felt like someone was sitting on this chest, there was nothing.

Next stop was the cellar. Everyone had to see the complete panic on my face when talking about the basement, and Kelly suggested we call it a night because it was getting late and Luke and I needed sleep. Karen, Kelly, and Mora had cots they would set up in the dining room and living room; they would take turns with the boys and have catnaps. I didn't think Luke or I would be able to sleep, but I barely remember my head hitting the pillow. Luke had a harder time as he could hear them talking indistinctly downstairs, but he finally felt safer than he had in a long time and fell into a deep slumber.

At 5:00 AM, everyone was up with the birds. Coffee was brewing, and the box of donuts I brought the day before lay opened on the kitchen counter. Today they wanted to study the footage taken throughout the night and just talk about anything I was willing to divulge to them.

Later during the day, they wanted to try to tackle the dreaded basement as a group. During this time, Luke was part of the discussions; he joined us outdoors, and we all went over the findings and details of the night before. I was thrilled to finally have a chance to talk about the house to people who were not going to judge me, people who had to have seen it all, and I would not be labeled certifiable. We told them almost everything.

Standing in the backyard, everyone gathered in a circle, noting that Luke was missing. We called out to him to join us, and he emerged from around the corner of the barn. He had blood across his left cheek and dripping down his neck.

"Oh my god, Luke! What happened to you?"

"I guess I was not welcomed in the barn again. Something is out to get me. I was pushed and slapped across the face. It was not just a slap. There were claw marks deep enough to draw blood." Luke was trying to act macho and undefeated, making a joke that maybe it would improve his appearance as he was just too good-looking before.

James had set up an energy counter and camera in the barn and ran to take a look at the monitor screen in the kitchen to see if anything was visible. Usually, anomalies would not show up with the camera as it was daylight, and the night vision cameras picked up the visuals. James called us all in to see and verify what he saw on the rewound footage. Luke's warm energy was bright and distinctive on the film, and right behind him closing in fast was a dark mist charging toward him, and as we watched him, the body pushed forward as his head twisted sideways.

No one wanted to show fear; they worked in the paranormal world and were professionals, like medical doctors who had to keep their emotions under control. It was clear that they had been taken aback and were worried about themselves and us. They came here to do a job, but they didn't plan to discover what they found and not so much of it. They usually would wait until darkness fell to continue with testing throughout the house. Still, obviously, in our case, it did not matter whether it was day or night, light or dark.

"If you are up to it, Augusta, will you come down to the basement with us now if we promise to keep you safe?

"Luke, let's clean you up first and have you relax on the couch. We will go over all our findings, suggestions, and recommendations going forward."

I could not believe I was going to the basement. I hit the dirt floor with James and Gordon ahead of the ladies and me right behind. The air was thin and damp and smelled like decay. I felt a wave of gaseousness come over me and felt dizzy. I was caught immediately by Karen and Kelly, holding each of my arms.

"Are you okay, Augusta? Do you want to go back up?"

"No," I said, "let's just get this over with and finished."

Everyone stood hand in hand in a small circle and was very still, waiting. Somewhere we could hear what sounded like growling and then moaning. I tried to relax by breathing through my nose and out my mouth, asking my heart to settle down and slow down. The rage that engulfed me was so intense.

Through my own eyes, I saw I was a man. I looked down at my armor-clad body. There was blood on my hands and on my knees. It was not my blood, but the blood of vengeance that I longed for from my enemies. I was carrying a knife in my right hand not yet satisfied as I felt my enemies' long sharp blade pierce my body.

I found myself sitting on the couch next to Karen who was holding my hand. Everyone was present and very concerned about my well-being. I asked what had happened and how I got upstairs. Karen said, "We brought you back up. We heard movement and load bangs upstairs. We heard yelling, and Luke asked us to come back upstairs, so we brought you back."

"Look at the dining room chairs, Augusta. Luke had witnessed them being tossed into the air like toothpicks while we were in the basement. Those wooden chairs are heavy, and to turn them over would require tremendous energy," Kelly said. "I believe that your life force of power was being attacked, drained."

Luke piped in, saying, "Possession?"

"Yes, in a way. We have been many places around the country, helping people, cleaning houses, and reporting our findings. This house is exceptionally active. We usually experience residual activity, but this is something different. We believe it is because of you, Augusta. The negative and positive energies, or ghosts as most people call them, have been here for a very long time and always will be because this place, like others around the world, has what we term magnetic energy. You, Augusta, can manifest them at a whole new level, which is not seen often. The energy field has always been here, but your presence seems to empower it enough for others to view and feel it also.

"We believe the second bedroom is holding Sarah. I think that is where she died. A young girl died in this house from some sort of stomach disease. The attic is where she played. Those items you found belonged to her, and we believe by taking them out of the house and cleansing that room with your help, we can assist Sarah to move on. Her presence is more substantial here than many of the others as she died here."

Mora added that Native American families once inhabited the land. They were hunter-gathers and later became farmers. They were no threat; they were peaceful people in life and after. "They see you, Augusta, as a white spirit ghost that is just part of their space. They do not even see or recognize Luke's presence."

"Mora said there is so much activity here. You have apparitions, color-filled orbs, shadows, noises, room temperature changes, physical contact, and poltergeist movement. In a short time, we have been here, we have experienced at least half of these paranormal events. We have K2 equipment activated, voice recordings, and laser grid beams broken. We even have a video showing unexplained shadows peaking around doors."

"James said he was not able to keep the batteries in his equipment charged. No matter what he did, the cells would just drain. I am suggesting that something else needs that energy. It would be like a car radio left on or a live hot wire loose in the ground, always drawing and using the electrical current. I have checked, and there are no electrical problems here."

"That tells me something. We even had to leave the van running as the low battery light was on."

James had the tape recorder and pressed play. At first, we only could hear static and indecisive noise, then there was a low demonic growl and a voice saying, "GET OUT! I WANT YOU OUT!"

Luke went into a panic and wanted to run out of the house immediately, but Kelly calmed him down and asked me to speak as she thought I had something to ask. I did not have anything to ask. I was talking out loud to myself.

Luke went to talk, and Kelly stopped him with an extension of her hand. She realized I had a revelation and was about to release.

Chapter 20

Revelation

"Familiar once-witnessed memories came to me too easy to comprehend all of them. Still, I realized they were flashbacks of my history, not only the history of this life but also many of the experiences I've led. The rage in the basement is that of a soldier who died in war, not yet done with his revenge. I am the sad little girl in the room upstairs in agony, afraid, sick, frightened, and dying alone. It was me being driven to my death in a blood-soaked wagon covered in urine, looking for my loved ones. I was the vision that the young Native American children saw as an apparition who met my ancestors in the woods by the river. There are so many lost souls all around me.   Now I know that Jonathan was the wise man, the more enlightened me who had entered those higher planes but had chosen to return and lead me in my search for understanding. He is here because I was looking for help. I am Jonathan for the others trapped here, searching for a guide to help them to let go and move on.

"I woke up this house, and in return, they did the same for me. I have always known, just like all of us, forgetting over time who we are and why we are here, that awareness is deep inside our DNA and our cells. I'm searching for the center of my labyrinth. My journey is searching for a different reality, other possibilities. I'm here to know, but there's a price to pay for it. I'm going to have to make a call if I can afford it.

"I'm so sorry, Luke. It's my entire fault. You have to know that I didn't want to hurt you. We all have energy inside us. Some can call it out upon demand and harness it. Obviously, I was not aware I was doing this throughout my life.

"Whenever I felt physically or emotionally threatened, I would unconsciously bring that energy forward in many forms, lashing out even if it meant waking up this house to protect me. When I felt overwhelming sorrow or compassion, the power would become something else. I would have visions of prediction, and I could escape by traveling to faraway places like taking a vacation or a trip to visit someone that needed help. When stressed, overworked, and not in balance, the energy would turn against me, making me sick and inducing pain, forcing me to wake up and listen.

"Rick, my temporary roommate, ended up in the hospital, suffering from the same affliction that killed Sarah, and it would have killed him.

"I didn't realize what was going on." The tears rolled over my face. "Subconsciously I have been angry with you. Even as a young child, I was told I was rebellious, unsettled, and searching for other truths. I always asked why over and over again. I knew there was more to life than what my parents, the church, and my teachers were telling me, and nobody could give me answers because they did not know they lived on faith and belief. I looked for the answers on my own. I must have opened up those doors very young in life. Then I physically died in that car accident, and in death as in life, I continued to ask and search for more knowledge, more truths, which opened up more doors and allowed the energy field in this place to find me and haunt me until I came. They called me because I asked, and I heard. The entities here are real. I have made them real."

I looked up from my rambling monologue to a dumbfounded group, just staring at me. Kelly was the first to react. "Augusta, it seems like you have had a very profound revelation. Now you have to decide on how you are going act on it. We can help some of the others move on that want peace. We do not feel that these entities in the house are a threat to you and your husband. You can all live together and, as you put it, learn and help one another. We feel though there are more dangerous ones here that are a threat. You do not have control of them. They are compelling, and I am sorry to say we have angered them.

"You asked us not to divulge the house or your identities, and we will not. We may use some of the voice recordings and pictures we have captured and write about our experience here, but no one will know about you or the location. If you need us or things get worse, we will come back. Augusta, you have a special gift. I think you can acquire more of the knowledge you seek outside of this house. It will not be easy to leave or break the bonds as you are part of this house, but you can do it."

I agreed some things were too precious to give up, even for knowledge.

Making the Break

We decided to put our Connecticut home on the market after only being there for two years. We started to look around for another home free of any felt energy. We did find a beautiful country farm home in the next town still close enough for me to drive to the university and for Luke to drive to his job. The farmhouse we wanted was on the market for a while, so we hoped we could sell our home before that one was gone. I wanted it, so I assumed that is where we would be eventually.

The realtor informed us that we had to disclose to any prospective purchaser that some people had experienced some paranormal activity. If we didn't do it and they didn't sign off on the disclosure and they were still willing to buy the house knowing that, we could be run into problems.

I knew that would not be a problem because just as the previous owner had to wait for me before the house let him go, I, too, had to wait for the next person with the calling, and if they had the calling, they would not care about any disclosures.

We were not surprised when the house was not cooperating when realtors came by with clients. We never got to the point of having to disclose anything. Electrical problems occurred where there was no explanation. There were water leaks, doors that did not correctly close, and the stench of death from the basement made its way up into the kitchen. Then an infestation of ladybugs arrived, taking over the house, covering every room on the days when there was supposed to be a showing. The realtors stopped coming when they started to get flat tires in the driveway, dead car batteries, or became deathly ill when entering the house.

One day, there was a knock on the door. The person's name will not be disclosed as I believe she still owns the home.

"Hi, I know I am supposed to go through a realtor, but I was hoping to see the house, and no one is calling me back. Would you mind if I looked around? If not, I understand."

I asked if she was indeed in the market to buy or just curious as we had a lot of that going on lately.

"Yes, I need a house. My husband is in the navy. I have a son who has just been enrolled in the Magnet School here, and I just got a job at the university in their catering department. I have been driving by this house for weeks, and I feel like I should be here."

I smiled and welcomed her in. I saw Luke crossing his fingers behind his back and walked away, letting me lead the way. She loved everything she saw, and surprisingly, nothing devious happened. The house was behaving itself, a good sign. We ended our tour outside on the back deck Luke had built overlooking the field and the reservoir. Our first genuine prospective buyer was awed by the magnificent views. She wanted to know why we were selling the house and why the price was below market value for the area. I clarified that we bought the house for an excellent price and that we already found a more significant place with a better-equipped barn for my horse and riding trails and that we priced the house to sell quickly so we didn't lose the other spot. I paused and said, "There is something else I have to disclose to you."

She stopped me. "I already know if you are referring to the spirits in this house. No need to explain. I feel them, and it is a good feeling. I have no problem with it. We can do this through our lawyers. I don't think we have to get any of the realtors involved, seeing that no one bothered to call me back."

"That is great! My contracts with them are over anyway, and I was trying to decide if I wanted to relist, but now I don't have to. I am so happy you stopped by. I will have our lawyer draw up the papers and contact your lawyer."

I kept my composure, and Luke was breaking at the seams with pure delight as she pulled out of the driveway.

As soon as the official offer contract was signed and the deposit received, we placed an offer on the farmhouse and began to pack. Luke had to keep an eye on me, worried about any retaliation I might get from the house. I began to feel really sick with high fevers and immobilizing depression. One day, my temperature hit 103 degrees.

Luke reached out to my mom, asking for help. She told him, "Luke, you need to finish packing the house yourself, and you have to get her out of there now! I will send up your brothers-in-law to help you, and you get Augusta to a friend's house or the B&B down the street until your new home is ready. Do not allow her to reenter the house again."

The new home closing was in three days, and I went to stay at the B&B down the street. It only took one day for my fever to break and my strength to return. Additional help came the day the moving van arrived to load all the boxes and furniture that we would keep for the next two days. The truck was backed up to the front door for quick loading, just like we did when we moved in, and everything was loaded. The boys sat on the front steps eating pizza and drinking beer pleased their day's work had been successful when suddenly they noticed the ground where the truck stood was giving way, and it was sinking! It sank right in front of their eyes in the soft dirt, all the way to the wheel wells. We believed this was a last attempt from the house to stop us. What a nightmare! The ground was not even wet. How could that have happened?

They'd have to call a tow to get it out of the hole in which it was sitting, and they worried after they pulled it out if it was going to leave a big mess. The next morning, there was going to be a walkthrough by the new owners. How would it be fixed in time? We already told them they could back their truck up to the door and unload their stuff.

With great effort, the box van was finally dislodged and parked in the driveway while all three of the guys worked on filling in the massive hole left behind. It was not perfect, but maybe they would not notice. We felt a little bad that the same thing would happen to them, but there was no going back now, and we selfishly thought at that point that the house would be theirs along with everything and everyone there. They agreed to take the home as is and signed off on all our disclosures.

The moving van was parked at the B&B the next day, and as we returned from signing the paperwork on our new home, we passed the house. There in front of the house was their moving van twice the size and weight as ours, and it stood perfectly fine. We saw no problems at all. The house had accepted them and let me go.

Moving On and Regrouping

The new farmhouse was beautiful and free from paranormal activities. Sonny and Muggsy were happy as were Luke and I. The mortgage was higher than we were used to. Still, Luke was a workaholic and had no problem taking on more hours at the casino, and I had worked my way up to the director of sales position with a significant pay increase. Employers tend to take advantage of competent workers, and we were motivated and liked having material things. We both allowed ourselves to be overworked and caught up in a fast-paced environment.

I should have known better by now that all of this brought on mental stress followed by physical illness. I fell into society's medical traps. Take this pill for this problem, which caused another problem. If I was not working,

I was hanging out in doctors' offices, having one test after another taking medication that was only masking the issues, not curing the problems or finding out what to do to prevent them. I was not a stranger to pain or sickness, and I conquered it before, and I was determined to do it again. I had to find other possible ways to get better because there are always other possibilities and answers. I was just not looking in the right place.

Chapter 21

Costa Rica

Luke and Augusta, over the years, visited Costa Rica a week to twelve days at a time. They kept going back whenever they could because Augusta called it her happy place. She felt strangely connected and would cry when it was time to leave. They built a vacation home, a small cabin so they would spend more time there, escaping the United States and work whenever possible. Luke said Augusta was a different person when there. Costa Rica was a place where she could quiet her mind, and things made sense there.

They would retire for the night very early because the cabin had no TV and no Internet. Augusta would get up every day before Luke at 3:00 AM just to write from her journals alone. She could sleep in because they were on vacation, but she did not. Augusta was writing in her journals again. There was a story she wanted to be share. Augusta started to write and meditate again, and she was content. They always had to leave though and go back to the rat race, which in time brought on more illness not just for her but also for Luke.

They were not getting any younger, and their lives were no longer theirs. They found themselves running the hamster wheel. All Augusta noticed was that she could write while in Costa Rica—it was the only place she could find inspiration. Her story was not being told and maybe never would be as years had passed and her illness became life-threatening, making it impossible to go to Costa Rica anymore, so they found themselves selling the cabin.

Luke took on more hours at work to pay the bills, and Augusta had to go on medical leave, desperately looking for the answers that no one could give them on why she was so sick. Augusta made a bold and risky decision to walk away from all conventional doctors and search within herself for answers. It was not her time to go, and she knew better than anyone the knowledge and path home was there. She had to look harder. This was her wake-up call. To ignore the request most likely would be the cause of her physical death.

Augusta found her answers stepping off the ordinary path. Her questions and answer came from a naturalist doctor who had her medical degree in internal medicine but believed in so much more and practiced Western and Eastern medicine together. She was more than just a doctor. She was extraordinary and not only helped Augusta heal physically but also believed people could cure themselves if they had the knowledge and mental strength to do so. She was able to remind her of the powers and the gifts she had forgotten we all hold. She had abandoned that part of herself when she got caught up in trying to find material happiness and neglected her personal journey.

The doctor and subsequent friend helped her get back on track just before the doctor's earthly life was ended in a bloody massacre orchestrated by her husband who was now waiting on death row and will have to return over and over again to that place until he gets it right. Augusta thought of her often as I am sure many still do. She touched so many lives.

Augusta finally quit her hotel job to take a position where she could use her talents but not be abused. She was lucky to find a place with a company and to make a new friend within her boss and a paycheck not as hefty as she was accustomed to, but it forced her to live a little less substantially and allowed her to focus more on her next earthly and spiritual journey.

Luke did the same. He was able to retire but still work for extra money, and they were learning together that there was indeed a new path for them.

I believe it was Buddha who said something like the following:

> "Man is the most confusing because he is willing to give up his health to make more money, and then he uses that money to fix his health. He doesn't live in the future or the present but lives like he is never going to physically die and so he ironically dies without ever living."

They spent a year studying, investigating, gathering paperwork, and downsizing their lives, preparing for their move to Costa Rica. Moving to another country is a lot different than going there on vacation, especially if you are planning on doing it right. If you plan on doing something like this, don't ask anyone for their opinion as they are burdened and plagued by the same limitations as you are. You have family and friends to deal with, and everyone has their own idea of why you are moving, and some feel you are deserting them. People are excited for you but ultimately frightened at the same time. Others think you are running away from something and don't understand why anyone would want to leave the best country in the world that has the most to offer any human being to go live in a second- or third-world country. Why make this bold change when you get older when your life should be more comfortable, not harder?

They would be right if those were any of the reasons for them leaving, but their journey in life was different than the ones they left behind. Augusta was searching for knowledge that could only be acquired by quieting her mind and by stepping out of her comfort zone. Augusta believed you cannot learn anything new if you do not challenge yourself and try new things no matter what age you do it. It takes time and determination to make this kind of change. It is complicated adjusting and emerging into another culture with a different language, different government and food, and surprisingly hard to live more simplistic.

Wrapping up the First Round

The first week they were settling in, Augusta was sitting on the couch when a breeze blew through. She looked at Luke and said, "Oh, smell that? Are those honeysuckles?"

"No, I don't think so. I do not know if Costa Rica has honeysuckle bushes here. I think it might be the *ylang-ylang* tree."

Many of Augusta's predictions since she first started writing in her journals in the early years before arriving in Costa Rica had already happened or were in the process of happening now, and the rest would follow fast. She continued to write in her journal. This might mean because she knew her life on this earth would be over soon as the world enters into a pandemic lockdown. Many have already died, and life as we know it will never be the same. She understood the urgency she felt having to move when they did and doing it the correct way. If they did not, they most likely would not have been able to at all as the countries locked down their borders, and getting settled would have been even more difficult if even possible at all.

There were goals she gave herself coming to Costa Rica, and she was working on them. The first goal was completing her journals. The second was to get as healthy as possible, which for a while worked. The third was to learn Spanish. The fourth was to look for and find Jonathan.

Augusta's Final Entries

What I bring with me to Costa Rica is the knowledge that is unique to me. Knowledge acquired is a gift that comes from suffering and living life outside of the ordinary. You can emerge from pain, confusion, and lost memories ready to start a new journey because your life experiences make you unique and prepared for the adventure on the road to come.

I understand a little bit more about who I am and why. I now know nothing has ever been taken from me. There has been no suffering I have experienced that did not come bearing a gift. We can all be taught STEM, the educational platform we all know as science, technology, engineering, and mathematics. STEM, I know from firsthand experience, can be lost or forgotten, but the experience and the knowledge that transforms a person is forever.

Now that I've settled in my new country and I've been able to relax my mind enough, I remember again the gift of vision to know when it is time to move on and step away from all things earthly that had served its purpose. I will say that I can keep digging for information that I can pass on to others who are looking for potential answers and listening.

Hello, Jonathan, it's nice to see you again. Let's talk.

CPSIA information can be obtained
at www.ICGtesting.com
Printed in the USA
BVHW030021141020
590973BV00001B/53

9 781664 128484